CU00868518

Coyote Redux

The Paleolithic Legend Lives!

Books by violet reason
  cheap visions
  retreads
  carbon dreams
  coyote redivivus
  waste heat

Books by Yulalona Lopez
  Tropomorphoses
  Night Wolves
  Coyote Remasked
  Coyote Rebooted
  Coyote Reloaded
  Coyote Recrude(scent)
  Coyote Recon(stituted)
  Coyote Renegade
  Coyote Refocused
  Coyote Recharged

Books from Calliope Press
  Musings, ed. by Crawford Washington
  Masks, ed. by Crawford Washington
  Wild Apples, by A. M. Caratheodory
  Amphibian Dreams, by A. M. Caratheodory
  Protected by Trees
  Forgotten Ruins
  Two Diaries, by Marcus Rian
  The Thesis, by Marcus Rian
  Lucifer Dreaming, by Marcus Rian
  Waiting for Better Times in Bulgaria, by Conor Ciaran
  Fragments, by A. M. Caratheodory
  Light from a Vanished Forest, by A. M. Caratheodory
  Gone Away

Coyote Redux

The Paleolithic Legend Lives!
—Industrial Strength Version—

The further frenetic mythopoetic adventures
of Coyote in post-modern civilization as he
steals a car, invents television, hunts a mouse,
runs for office, and meets interesting new people
like—you know, important people, actors and
politicians and such—Death, Forest Trump,
Baglady, Bombay Chevrolet, Sam McHooter,
Legba, and the New Young Modern Gods.

violet reason
Yulalona Lopez

Coyote Redivivus Series
Volumes 1-2

Calliope Press
Sarasota
2016

Acknowledgments

Several of these works have been published on internet sites; several have been published in earlier versions in earlier books. Sixteen more Coyote stories were assembled from violet reason's notes and expanded by Yulalona Lopez, who added the last twenty four original stories of her own. Lopez can be reached at Yulalona@3muses.us

Graphics by Ryan Garcia Calusa
Moscow, Idaho
design@riangarciacalusa.com

copyright © 2005 2007 2016 by A. M. Caratheodory
All rights reserved under International and Pan-American Copyright Conventions. No part of this book may be used or reproduced in any manner without written permission from the Publisher, except in the case of brief quotations embodied in articles or reviews.

Publishers Cataloging-in-Publication data
Violet Reason, 1945-2004
Yulalona Lopez, 1969-
Coyote Redux/violet reason & Yulalona Lopez
I. Title.
PS3553.A644A898 2016

ISBN-13: 978-1518768064 (paper)
ISBN-10: 1518768067

3 Muses Books / Calliope Press
   Sarasota, Florida, editor@3musesbooks.com
Mozart & Reason Wolfe, Limited
   Wilmington, Delaware, mozart@reasonwolf.com

Manufactured in the United States of America

First Edition
3 4 5 6 7 8 9 10
(Third Printing)

Approximate Contents

Three Perspectives

Ms. Alma Beangurd (Editor of this volume): "Professor Snootwhistle, would you please begin our enlightened discussion of Coyote?"

Prof. Snootwhistle (Yale Professor of Mythology): "Coyote is a vulgar but sacred form of the trickster character that exists in many human cultures. The trickster scandalizes, disgusts, amuses, disrupts, chastises, and humiliates the animal people of the protohistorical era, yet he is also humiliated by them, as he is undermined by his own greed and thoughtlessness. Trickster Coyote is a creative force who transforms the peopled world, in bizarre and outrageous ways, with his cunning and boundless energy. His constant scavenging for food represents the most basic animal instincts. But, he is also the spiritual father of the true people and a conduit for spiritual forces to them in the form of sacred dreams.

"What an ambiguous, ambitious, ambidextrous creature he *is*! Cunning personified, a magician, a cheat, yet through his overweening curiosity and his tendency to meddle in things of which he lacks real knowledge, he often makes a fool of himself. He steals fire but burns his fingers. Caught in contradiction, he lives by his wits, yet he falls into traps set by mice and birds. He subversively disrupts conventions, and crosses forbidden boundaries, yet he displays no overtly high, solemn purpose in these activities. He's a god, but a god of dirt and manure, and of shameless, unsanctioned sex. He's a teller of lies, but of lies without malice. He just lies in order to cover up his thefts, simple thefts driven by a motive of simple appetite, or simply for the fun of stealing, or merely to fool people, or to concoct interesting stories, or to stir things up when they get dull. He tell his lies with charm and playfulness, with an abandon that affirms the pleasure of fabulous fabrication.

"In every culture that has a trickster god, where the other gods embody perfection, the trickster makes mistakes that bring about change, always the opposite of his intentions, either through a horrible mess or with a joyful expression."

Ms. Beangurd: "Thank you Professor Snootwhistle, for a positive and erudite introduction to Coyote. Doctor Roegrimes, what do you have to add?"

Dr. Harold Roegrimes (Independent Scholar of the History of Science):
"Snotthistle, you idiot. Coyote is evil. No ambiguity there. No doubt at all. His lies cause real people to die real deaths, and not just in fun or temporarily, but permanently. His falseness causes great suffering, real suffering, not just entertaining stories or news items.

"Coyote is not a trickster, he is a psychopath, a psycho who hates good people, as well as truth and order. He is not some mythical gatekeeper who opens doors to the spirit world powers for people. He pretends to be so only so he can get away with his wretched mischief. We may live in a dual reality of good and evil, but he is one pole, the evil, pure negativity. He fools us by seeming so innocent, but he is evil. We rationalize that he is a scapegoat for our flaws and self-hatred, but he is the cause of those things, the teacher of irresponsibility, the mentor of hate and lust, the dark side of the farce. It is the dark side that we must deny, learn from and deny, and not praise and emulate."

Prof. Snootwhistle: "Listen, Roadgrime you dildo, if you had half the publications I do—"

Ms. Beangurd: "Gentlemen, please, don't get personal. Let me make a short statement and then we may continue. You're both wrong.

"Coyote is not really a trickster at all. He is not really a representative of dualisms like generosity and greed—there were no, are no, such dualisms in nature; that is a western Aristotelian distinction. As a creator of order out of chaos and a destroyer of order, an animal being and a spiritual force, Coyote seems contradictory and ambiguous, but that is a human perceptual limit. There is no difference between the animal we see as a coyote in the field, and the personification of Coyote power in all coyotes, the Being of the being so to speak, between the trickster in tales and the symbolic character of disorder in the myths.

"Coyote is not evil, either. Such evil is another recent cultural judgment. Coyote simply is, like a tree. Even a tree may fall and kill a squirrel or block a stream, but that is not evil. Coyote is a physical entity onto which we can project good or evil, but there was no distinction in the past; Coyote simply was and is. What we think of as evil can result in good, just as good actions can have evil consequences. Over lifetimes, the concepts of evil and good, as well as their definite actions become so intertwined, we cannot ever tell which things were good or evil or which caused good or evil. Of course, there is no simple cause and effect, either.

"Coyote is a locus of ideas. Coyote is a complex of images, from which one can learn many lessons, regardless if the world is Aztec, Hopi or industrial Michigan. He is a survivor who uses his wits and instincts to adapt to the changing times. He appears in many guises as an adaptive god, sensitive to changes in the world. That is why these stories can be updated to the modern world. As the authors, Miss Reason and Miss Lopez, have done. We can learn from these stories of Coyote reborn. Yes, professor, please respond."

Prof. Snootwhistle: "Doctor Boredgrind, if you really have such a degree, you would understand that Coyote, the trickster, teacher, survivor, and fool, has inhabited this continent much longer than the later arriving humans from Asia, who have only been here about 13,000 years or so, and far longer than your late-guest ancestors from England. Coyote, with wolves and dogs, was born here.

"Miss Beeturd, you simple twit, Coyote is nothing but a trickster, who obviously has tricked you into believing that he is not.

"Now, that said, Coyote is a figure who defies category, at once the scorned outsider and the inner cultural hero, the mythic transformer and the buffoon, a creature of low purpose and questionable habits who establishes precedent, dabbles in the creation of the world that will be, and provides tools, food, and clothing to the people who inhabit that world.

"He thrives in a region where ambiguity, paradox, and confusion are the natural order, where opposites commingle. He straddles the juncture of two worlds, belonging to neither and yet to both. This region is a potent source of creation. He is the inflated avatar of this region of boundaries and possibilities. He is the shaman of order and disorder.

"Coyote seems self-seeking and haphazard, but that is the source of his power. By acting true to character, the trickster performs a shamanistic ritual that connects the other world to the world of the people through acts of creation and transformation that we recognize in the world of myth. Coyote achieves mythic success through lust and impatience, and fortunate accident. His goals are not realized; he is only the conductor of forces that he puts into motion, but other things that are good and useful come to be. Failure is transformed into success; on the mythic level he performs the most significant feat of destroying the inviolability of all that is sacred or secret.

"Your limited religious perspective cannot pierce the trickster's mythic core, for it dwells deeply in the landscape in which he travels and performs. If we are to begin to understand the trickster, and to perceive the strange unity that arises from his contradictory irrational nature, we must examine him as a function of this landscape, and furthermore as its haphazard and unconscious manipulator."

Dr. Roegrimes: Oh, Snorepistol, you sad, deluded romantic hack. Beanguard, you ignorant scientist. Coyote is absurd. Yes, and the shaman is an absurd creature, like Coyote, trying to channel animal power to help people. He is a powerful, unpredictable, and incomprehensible outsider who creates and balances by accident and ignorance. The shaman, accompanied by assistant spirits, tries to fetch the souls of sick persons from the realm of the dead. He fails. The dead are dead.

"Coyote is antisocial, cowardly, and unsavory, even if infinitely entertaining to buffoons like you, comfortable academically-insulated buffoons. His evil is well-known to the people, and wherever he goes everyone knows who he is and what he is, and they avoid him like the rabid little mutt he is. Coyote pretends to be a powerful shaman, but his powers are flawed, his spells are incomplete, and he creates more suffering, not just normal suffering, but awful, intense suffering caused by interference. That is another evil, the interference, beyond the selfish joy in causing pain.

"In some native traditions, Coyote impersonates the creator, making humans out of mud and bringing into being the buffalo, elk, deer, antelope, and bear. But, these beings bear the imprint of the false god, and never lead to good endings."

Prof. Snootwhistle: "Listen Crowrhymes, I'm sick of your superior chattering claptrap—"

Dr. Roegrimes: "Beancurd, do something to keep this wetdream limp in his sock, or I wi—"

Ms. Beangurd: "I do not appreciate this kind of bickering. As editor, I will edit out anything else except my conclusion, so bite down hard on it, boys.

"Too often we consider Coyote as a mythic symbol, polymorphous pervert, or simply a good story, but in fact Coyote exists in an ecological context as a scavenger and predator in many kinds of ecosystems, wild ones, artificial ones, agricultural areas, and suburbs. The creature coyote resembles a medium-size dog with a narrow face, tawny fur and a bushy tail, which is carried straight out below the level of its back. Coyotes found in low deserts and valleys weigh about 20 pounds; those in mountains or cities can weigh up to 50 pounds. Desert coyotes are light gray or tan with a black tip on the tail. Coyotes of high elevations have fur that is darker, thicker and longer; some specimens have a white tip on the tail. In winter the coats of mountain coyotes become long and silky, and trappers still hunt them for their fur.

"Coyotes are opportunistic feeders, singly of mice, in packs of larger prey. They are omnivorous feeders; they prey on small animals, eat plant matter, carrion, and garbage. Their canid hunting style is partly determined by their slow-twitch muscle fibers, which require oxidative metabolism of fats. Thus, rather than always stalk their prey and pounce, Coyotes can run down their prey. In fact, Coyotes get pleasure from the hunt itself, which can be a social activity, and they will run for pleasure even when not hungry. Sometimes, like wolves or dogs, they will stalk and chase symbolic prey, like sticks or pinecones.

"Coyotes are an invaluable part of a healthy ecology and environment, which sustains all life, including that of domestic livestock and humans. A high density of food sources allows coyotes, who normally have large home ranges of many square kilometers, to thrive in areas as small as a 100 acres. Thus, more Coyotes can occupy a large area, with less need to defend their territories.

"This small prairie wolf has attracted the interest of native peoples, who hung roles on her, as well as the deadly attention of ranchers and biologists, concerned with exterminating the species. The coyote lives on the border of human domains. As such, Coyote represents the border to humans, and is a useful symbol of change and adaptation. A border joins the cosmos and the world of the people in a whole culture, and represents change. A society that moves from hunting and gathering to an agricultural way of life, for example, experiences a complex interaction of thresholds that range from the larger transitions in technology, ritual, mythology, and art to the reaction of a single member of that society to the introduction of a new tool or novel mythological theme.

"Coyote provides a recognizable point of interaction with the invisible worlds of death and the supernatural. That is what Coyote is, a mask that we can put on and look towards the invisible or large, a pelt that we can hang human foibles on, a story that we can tell our children that lets them learn without being forced to learn. Biologically, Coyote has thrived in the face of destruction; culturally, Coyote is relevant to our modern behavior. The authors here show us how."

Coyote Remembers

Coyote turns Or a Native American love story

A woman in the village, plain and lonely
saw a dog chase by her home;
the dog was handsome and healthy;
she wished for him, Coyote.

That night, he turned into a man
and came to her door, to be husband
to her— "Never tell anyone what you saw,
never mention it at all."

They lived together many years,
quarreled and fought and loved;
she never again thought of his origin,
long becoming used to him.

But one day they saw some local
mutts all chasing after a bitch
everywhere here and everywhere there,
without pause, around them.

She remembered what he had been
and asked him if he wanted to be that
again—and he said 'yes' and turned away
and ran toward the others to play.

Coyote cosmogenesis Or *Making water*

First, nothing made water
then water made Coyote
    then Coyote made water
then Coyote laid down and made land;
    he shit and made mountains
then he farted and clouds and air appeared
then he scratched his fleas and the land was populated
with fungus, plants, birds, animals, and people
    then everything was ready for Coyote
Coyote redivivus, Coyote redux,
Coyote man, Coyote woman.

And Coyote joyed in his world
    mixing, testing, changing,
fooling around with every possibility,
every emotion, need, or wild idea,
taking them apart, recombining them,
    interacting, interfering, entering
every play and event and scenting
it with Coyote odor, then sniffing,
sleeping, and dreaming—
    what Coyote created at once
he destroys piece by piece.

Smell of the Past Or *Raven Tree*

Nothing revives the past so completely as a smell!
Nothing goes faster from the nose bulbs to the brain bulbs.
It's hard-wired. It deals with dear sex, moods and fear of sex.
Coyote remembered his simple times as a young trickster,
when he was teaching the animals to adapt to a world
with monsters and humans.

Now he couldn't even smell. It was cold. The bitter wind
was whipping down the hills. It was like winter and Coyote
was really cold. He found a hollow tree and shouted "Open up,
dammit!" The tree did open and he crawled in to get warm.
He said, "Shut up, stupid," and it did. He was warm
and fell asleep — slept for months it seemed.
    Then it was warm and he wanted out. "Open up, now, woody,"
he demanded but the tree did not move. Coyote started yelling.
Coyote kept yelling until Woodpecker landed and made
a small hole near his eye. The echoing made Coyote's ears hurt.
Then the beak aimed for his eye, which looked like a juicy
round grub. Coyote squeezed his eyes shut. Woodpecker flew
away frustrated. Coyote's eye was black. He howled and kicked
the tree.
        That attracted the attention of Sapsucker, who drilled
another small hole by Coyote's ear.
        Coyote shouted at the bird, "Quit making that noise! I am
Coyote, trying to get out!! I do not belong here!!!"
        Eventually Razorcut Woodpecker came and made a large
hole by Coyote's stomach, pulling a few hairs, which looked
like worms, from Coyote's fur. Coyote screamed, but it did no
good.
        Finally, he had to realize that he could tear himself apart
and pass the pieces out of the hole. He cut off his tail,
and pushed it out. Then one leg and the other. Then his intestines.
Then an arm. Suddenly, Crow came along and flew off with the
intestines.
            "Stop that! Crow, stop!! I am Coyote!!!"
        But Crow said, "Why throw this away? This is good. Are you

crazy?" And he flew off anyway.

Coyote pushed the last pieces through, his head pulled last by the last arm. Then he had to put himself together and reach one arm with the other. Almost whole, he started looking for food.

The field near the tree had been burned, so he had some grasshoppers. That was why he had gotten warm. It was still fall!

From the tree, Squirrel shouted a warning. "Coyote, you are dropping grasshoppers from your ass!"

Coyote answered, "You eat raw nuts! What do you know!" And he kept eating. Then he saw squirrel was right and used some tree sap to plug his hole. Stupid Crow had his intestines. He kept eating the sparking grasshoppers until he heard Squirrel again.

"You're spilling a lot of smoke now from your ass!"

Coyote could feel the burn now. He howled and raced for the river before he burst into flames, but he got caught in some dense blackberry bushes and burned up completely before he got to the stream.

Crow dropped the last bits of intestines under his tree. The smell attracted Fox the next day, who recognized the smell, the essence of Coyote as it were, and jumped over them. The Great Spirit had charged Fox with reanimating Coyote whenever he was killed by a monster. Fox was unclear about the call on bad judgments, but he realized that Coyote himself was a kind of a monster.

Coyote was miraculously reborn and immediately started climbing the tree to get at Crow without even thanking his friend and savior.

Fox shook his head and continued hunting.

An Ultralight Romance Or Cloudcoyoteland

Coyote remembered some of his favorite runs when he had
teamed with other coyotes to catch a deer. He could feel
the slow-twitch muscle fibers pulling oxygen from fat cells
as he entered a zone of automatic strides. He looked ahead
at the shadow of the cloud he was trying to catch. What would his
mate Mole think when he came back with a mouth full
of cloud?

Coyote's mantra was: Food sex sleep. He was saying
his mantra as he loped along. Coyote had had a number of wives
already in his wifetime. He always wanted to marry someone or
something. He was getting closer to the cloud now, running up a
hill.

This cloud looked very beautiful, soft, white, gentle,
and nonjudgmental—also, deep, complex, and nonjudgmental.

Coyote jumped but could not reach her. He asked Hummingbird
for help, but Hummingbird knew he could never lift Coyote,
even an inch. But, he wanted to help and he had seen some
contraptions that might be of use to a clever dog. "I think
they are called ultralights. They fly low and are buzzy
and unstable. They hang out with the bigger metal birds
on a hard rock field."

Coyote was off to the races. He started to
form a Patrick Swayze face to get into the flight area of the airport.
It wasn't quite right, but he had a lot of hair. For some reason, the
masks of celebrities received much more respect and were more
useful than any original mask. And the masks of handsomer ones
were more productive than plainer ones.

He asked the owner and was able to get a free lesson if he signed
a few autographs.

He got in the go-cart and Ronnie showed
him how to start the engine. Then Ronnie laid out the inflatable
cloth wing and gave him instructions on how to steer it,
"Don't worry if the engine quits—you'll just glide down. Are
you ready?"

Coyote barked an assent and was ready for ascent.

The first day, he was able to fly up and see Cloud eye to eye
so to speak. He finally found the cloud—at least he thought
it was her. When he got close, though, she fell apart.

Then he turned around and slowed the ultralight. "I love you,"
Coyote said to Cloud. "I want to marry you."

The cloud scutted faster, replying "I can not marry you. I'm a
changeling. I am soft and fluffy, now, but I can become deep and black,
or grey, thin and ragged. You would have a hard time loving me then."

"My emotions build up like storm clouds. No, look, I am a
cloud myself," Coyote put pieces of cotton over his nose and eyes.
But he couldn't see, and the machine lost altitude, and he hit
his nose on the frame and couldn't smell his ass scent.

The cloud slowed, "I never saw a cloud fall so fast, unless
it was raining."

"Look," Coyote pointed to the blood on his shoulder,
"it's dark rain. Please let me marry you," Coyote insisted. "I will love
you even when you are ragged. I can hold you together through
every storm."

Then the hour was up and he was almost out of gas,
"I'll come back tomorrow!" Coyote shouted as he turned around and
accidentally dispersed Cloud again with the fan.

The next day, Coyote snuck into the airfield and stole the craft.
He found Cloud over the Arizona desert. "Hey, look," he said,
slowing down carefully and putting on a mirror mask.

Cloud loved that.

The third day, Coyote could not find her, or any clouds.

On the fourth day, Coyote and Cloud were
married by King Stratus.

She said, "I will call you Mahpiya Luta."

"And, I will call you Eidola. What does that Mahpiya mean?"
Coyote asked, playing with his mirrors.

"Red cloud," she replied, knowing that 'Eidolon' meant cloud.

Red? On the whole, though, Coyote was pleased. They
floated together for many days. They floated in the warm blue skies
and they floated in the cool starry nights. Well, she floated;
he had to go gas up every hour or two.

But one day the wind came and Cloud started to break up
into small pieces. Poor Coyote did not know what to do.

18

He began flying from one small cloud piece to another,
but soon had nothing to grab or see; the flying machine ran out
of gas and drifted to the ground.

He landed on a pebble beach by Dry Wash and was knocked
out cold. He lay on the rocks for several hours. Flies came
and settled around his mouth. Later that day a group of children
came down to the beach to play.

"Look! A dead dog!" one
of the girls called when she found Coyote's body lying flat
and still on the ground. The other children gathered around him.
They were shocked to see Coyote's face, with cuts and pieces
of mirrors.

Some of the children started to cry. "Poor dead dog,"
they crooned. "Poor dead dog."

One of the children put her pretty blanket over Coyote.
They left to tell their friends so they too could see the bloody, cut,
twisted, dead animal.

Rock Hard Loving

When Coyote woke up, he was alone. He sat down on a large rock
and thought and thought. 'I will never marry a cloud again.
I will never marry a gull or a raven or anything that flies.
I will not marry a rainbow or a star. From now on I will stay
on the ground, well, or under the ground.'

Coyote stood up and looked at the sky. Cloud was becoming
full and fluffy again, but he knew it could not work. He waved
to her, but she did acted aloof and not stop.

The rock was getting warmer. Coyote was wearing the
blanket, and got hot. He put it over the rock and said, "Here young
lady, you may have my fine blanket."

The rock noticed how fine it was with bright beads,
straight porcupine quills, and feathers that moved in the breeze.

Then it got breezy again and Coyote wanted it back.
He asked, but the rock, whose name was Raquelle, said, "No!"
He stole it away, but Raquey chased him. He took shelter up
the only tree in the field, and shouted to the rock, "Go away. It's my

blanket."

"But, you gave it to me!" Raquelle said. "It's an engagement gift."

Coyote thought a moment and said, "Will you marry me?"
Then Raquelle said, "Yes!"

Coyote asked if it was safe to come down. He wondered what their kids would look like.

That union with Rock only lasted a day, well, an hour, maybe two minutes. Anyway, he left, sore and bruised. And humbled. He walked for days, then collapsed, and slept for days. He was observed by two crows, the Crow Brothers, who were spying on Coyote. "Look at him, just lying in the sun, dozing off. Too much trouble to turn over or rearrange his legs. Why isn't he looking for food, like Mouse, or cleaning his fur, like Mountain Lion?"

"Yea, or observing cool animals like us? I'll tell you why. It's because Coyote is monumentally, appallingly lazy."

"Yea, I'm getting bored just watching him. How many hours has it been?"

"11,417."

"No, just today."

"Almost 4. Let's fly."

"Okay!"

And they flew off towards something shiny in the distance.

20

Crow favors Coyote

Coyote woke up and wandered. Later, he came upon Crow,
Kagihiga, who was talking across at pond at other crows.
Then, he heard his name, "Coyote, I need a husband for my sister,
Princess Du'bL'Dkup. You are the chosen one. What do you say?"

Coyote licked his lips and then nibbled them, what to do,
what to do?

Crow made a really loud call, "*Bracckkkk*," and two young
maidens stepped through the trees.

Coyote was dumbfounded by their grace and beauty.

The younger one approached Coyote and said, "I am Princess
Kudl'mi and this is my sister Princess Du'bL'Dcup. Will you come
home with us, to be our destiny?"

Coyote was a gentlemen's 'c' kind of guy, but he nodded.

Coyote could not speak, he just nodded and held out his hand
for them to grab. The girls brought him home. Their mother,
an old crow, but younger than Coyote, sized up the situation and said,
"You must eat first. You will need strength for what lies ahead."

Coyote nodded smiling, thinking he knew exactly what lay
before him.

"Now, feast on these wonderful dry artichoke roots first."

And Coyote did. Then, she dished out the beaver tail soup,
which was very fat indeed. He ate it right up, since it tasted
so good to him. Hours later, the old woman had gone.

Then Coyote went into the teepee with a long candle,
and when he reached the princess, she blew the candle out.
So he lay next to her. He said to her, in his most romantic way,
"You are a beautiful sea mammal. I want to hump you.
You have classic gas station architecture, I want to pump you.
After all, if you have a great idea, you have to spread it."

"What are you thinking of spreading?" the maiden asked shyly.

"Your legs and tail."

"Rest first," she cooed, "so we can
become accustomed to one another."

Later that night, her sister came in, disrobed and lay down.

Coyote thought, 'oh, balls, this night a legend will be made.'

The girls asked him to lie between the two of them, so

he did. Just as he fell asleep, his guts let out a terrible roar
and he defecated.

    "Oh dear," said Kudl'mi, "he's had a large bowel
movement. We don't want him to be embarrassed, so we should
change the bedding without waking him."

 But before they could do anything, he dumped another big load.

    "Oh no," said Du'bL'Dcup, "a larger deposit, this is too
much to touch, we need to wake him."

 .So they woke him up, but just as his eyes opened, unexpectedly
the voice of the old woman came from under the platform
where she had been hiding: "Oh no, the visitor has soiled
the princesses. Coyote trickled and dumped on the girls!"

    Kagihiga heard that and ran down the center of the village
yelling, "Coyote shit on our princess! Awful! Look, look at this!"

Of all the things that he had done in the past, few had embarrassed
Trickster, but this time he felt humiliated. He jumped up and ran off,
trailing brown spots.

    Kagihiga summarized it to the tribe: "Although
filled to the brim with brimborion, he is a fimetarious fadger."

 "What? What does that mean?" Chief Nobl'brow asked.

 "It means he lives in shit and is uselessly charming," smiled Crow.

Coyote was so ashamed he went to hide. He just lay in bed and
would not eat. Crow had done this to him on purpose.
Crow knew in advance that he was coming, that is why he gave
him artichokes and had a fat beaver tail fixed for him.
He did all of this just so Coyote could not contain himself.
He should have thrown it at the witnesses. Crow did this
out of jealousy, because he knew that Coyote was the better
Trickster and was about to get seriously laid. This is what made
him feel worse, not getting the right tail.

Magpie showed up later, and said, "Guy, why are you acting
this way? You are one of the greatest baddest ones ever created.
You should not feel sad."

    Coyote finally spoke and said, "I know, but
Crow has made me feel badder, because of my bladder." Then he
told Magpie everything that had happened.

Magpie said, "I knew it all along—this is why my heart is sore. It should not have been, as all creatures have abused you before, but Crow was one of the great ones created with you. You must get even quickly. I think I have an idea to rob him of his feathers."

"Really?" Coyote asked.

Magpie lowered his voice and continued: "Have Crow pose for you. Appeal to his vanity. And then, when ... mumble breezle ..."

Coyote Paints Crow

Coyote dressed as a middle-aged woman and set up a studio teepee in Crow's village. He said he would paint portraits of everyone, but Crow had to be first, as befit his status.

When Crow agreed, he gently persuaded Crow to take off his feathers to pose, "Can we accept that mystery? Accept not knowing things even things we have named and classified? Seeing nothing and understanding nothing, how can we survive? Can we survive with a poetic appreciation? We only need to look at our feet to see some connection or hear a brief note. We do not do all the weaving together; other things act on others. Heroic design and extravagance in life is needed. It is not contradictory or antithetical to frugal lifestyles or for restoring a healthy environment. Life is exuberant; energy is used, lives are lived and used, not saved. The reverse of shadow is a ray of light. Shed your shadow now, famous Crow!"

And Crow took off his feathers, and Coyote painted up a storm.

"You are an artist working in dung. Art is sacred, universally sacred," admired Crow.

Then Coyote told Crow to wait for the media to dry. He went outside and had Horse drag off the studio teepee, and Crow was naked under a few peacock feathers, surrounded by dung.

"Behold the drag queen!" Coyote shouted to the village.

Crow had no feathers and could not fly off—he had to run like a chicken, his skin turning pink with shame.

Coyote basked in his triumph.

Coyote decided to go home to Mole. No more clouds or rocks,
no more young, immature women. So, he started loping home.
However, he soon came across three young women bathing
and asked to join them. They said yes, but then he tried to fondle
their breasts inappropriately. One said cleverly, "Lie down little
god and I will take fleas out of your fur."
    Coyote lay in the sun, but became so relaxed he fell asleep.
When he woke up his hair was twisted around with cockleburs.
His ear was pulled to one side with both eyes. His thighs
were stuck together. He jumped and tripped and rolled.
    He heard one young woman hiding behind a tree say,
"That's the Cocklebur Trot!" Then he heard giggling.
He was angry but could not run or jump. He flopped around
trying to get his knife out. He had to cut out a lot of hair
to release the burs. He cut himself sometimes and was bleeding.
    He went back to his village to get help. But, then suddenly
he met his wife on the path—thinking quickly, he said,
"Oh, dear Mole you are alive! I had heard you were dead,
so I mourned you by pulling out my hair and cutting my skin
with sorrow. But, my suffering paid off. You are alive!"
    Mole raised her eyebrows. "Such bad news, and I am so lucky
to have someone as devoted as you. Come, let me bind your
self-inflicted wounds."
    She had to use a lot of alcohol from
fermented berries, and Coyote's screams woke up many innocent
sleepers.

MechHawk

Coyote needed to eat to get back his strength, especially
from Mole's gentle ministrations. He was about to scrabble
for a mouse when he had an inspiration.
He loped back to the Azport airport and approached the hanger
with a quick crude John Wayne mask. That would inspire trust
with the old owner.

"Hey, you're famous," said the owner, whose
name was Jack Wayne. "Look at these beauties, got 'em with
the insurance money. Some thief—

"Could I try that LightHawk over there?" Coyote asked.
"Sure, I guess. Need a credit card first," Jack peered at the short
customer.

Coyote took off cautiously, wanting to impress Jack.
Now he could hunt like hawk, like a bird, like eagle or vulture.
He could see his prey from above, what no other Coyote
on earth had ever done. So this is getting high he thought.
Coyote did not have 20/5 vision like Hawk, and he was a few
million photoreceptors short, but he had studied Hawk
and knew the moves. He drifted lower and slower,
then saw Rabbit running for a bush.

He zoomed straight down, but Rabbit went under a tree.
Coyote tried to pull up but the ultralight did not respond
quickly and he crashed beezer-first into the soft loam.

Sputtering with disappointment, he snuck back to the hanger
and pushed out the White kestrel model, careful not to interrupt
Jack as he watched reruns of *Married with Children*. Jack seemed to be
comforted by watching a husband worse off than he was.

Coyote almost went in to watch it, but he was hungry
and frustrated now.

He approached the canyon with the light in front of him.
He was sure someone would be drinking from the stream.
He cut the engine and glided down. He saw a mouse and tried
to start the engine, but the ultralight hit a boulder
and Coyote went flying into the sand, scraping his chest and legs.
He felt himself: Not killed, still conscious.

The mouse came over and looked, nodded sympathetically,

and asked, "Hey, Coyotelyodel, I wonder if I could do that."
      Coyote felt like one of the unluckiest predators around.

He wandered back to Mole, almost getting a mouse on foot.
Then he saw her and Fox hunting together, and he saw a redman
approach them, tentatively and cautiously.
He decided to watch, maybe get a few mice already stunned.

Legend of the Giant White Beaver

A young hunter of the Tohono O'odham just could not get a deer
or even one of the ranch bison. He sat and watched as a coyote
and a fox caught mice on another hill, the coyote diving
from above and stunning her prey, and the fox sidling up
and pouncing at the last minute. They seemed to be having
a contest about who could throw the mouse the furthest
and still recapture it before it could burrow to safety.
He approached slowly and respectfully. When they stopped
and sat, he started his story, "Can you help me? I cannot hunt.
I cannot attract a woman, I cannot make tools. I cannot do anything
right."
      Fox spoke, "You are asking correctly."
        Mole shook her head, "You remind me of someone."
    "Who? Everyone calls me Unlucky."
        "Was there a time," Fox asked, "when you may have killed
a white squirrel? That is punishable with bad luck."
      The young hunter stood with his mouth open.
        Mole was not surprised, and said, "There is something
you can do to change your luck. Listen to me and someday your
heart will be glad." She gave him a dead mouse, "take this food
to eat, for you must travel far down the river until you come
to a village of giant beavers. No! Stop smiling; this word
had a dignified formal meaning in my day. You will know
this is your destination by the size and fineness of their lodges.
Stand in front of the largest one, in respectful silence
for a long time, then sing the song I will teach you now.

26

When you have finished the singing, the chief of all the Beavers
in the world, a Great White beaver, will come to you.
He is wise, and will tell you what to do. You must do it
without asking why. Now go, and be brave!'

The young man started at once, although it was late in the day.
He walked with the long steps of youth, passing two human
Places and three small beaver villages, each too small
to be the right one. He traveled through the night. He ate
the no-longer-fresh meat. He kept going even though he was tired.
On the third day, he came upon a large lake, and he knew
there must be a large dam holding it. He saw regular willow
stumps beaver-cut. Then, he saw several great lodges, larger
than any he had ever seen. Then, he saw one that towered
above the rest, built from great trees, surrounded by bare ground.
This must be the lodge that he sought. He stood still until the sun
was low, then he sang the song.
          Soon a great white Beaver, as white as winter snow,
came to him and asked: "Why did you sing that song, my brother?
I have never heard one of you sing that before. Are you troubled?
What do you want of me?"
                    "I am Unlucky," the young man replied. "I
can do nothing well. No woman will marry me. My bow breaks
before I can hunt food for my family. My medicine is bad. I cannot
dream. My people pity me as they would a sick child."
          "First, you must think positively. You are not negatively
Unlucky, you are positively Screwed. I am sorry for you,"
said the White Beaver, "but I can do nothing for you myself. You must
find my brother, the White Bison, who knows where Old-man's lodge
is. The White Bison will do your bidding if you sing that song when
you see him. It is a long journey, so take this stick with you, and keep
it in your hand, so you can cross any river and not drown. Go, now."
and he waddled back to his lodge to watch television.

Then Unlucky/Screwed traveled down the river, more slowly,
now. He saw a rope bridge in the distance but decided to use
the traditional means and held the stick to float across
the two-foot deep river with a weak current. The sun was low
in the west on the fourth day, when he saw a White Bison alone

on a hillside near by. After looking at Bison for a long time,
the young-man commenced to sing the song.

When he had finished, the White Bison rumbled up close
to him and asked: "What is the matter? Why are you singing
that old song? To irritate me, to trouble me?"

Screwed told the White Bison what he had told the White
Beaver, and showed the stick to prove it. "I'm hungry, too;
I have not eaten for days."

"There is plenty of grass and tubers to eat.
Sit by the stream and cool your feet and rest." The Bison went off to
eat and came back in the morning. "I can do nothing for you,
but take this old arrow from my back and give it
to the White Coyote, the Old-man in his Lodge, who lives
over the mountain, in a tumble-down lodge in a smelly cave.
Go now and honor Coyote."

The young man walked across the plains towards
the mountains. The White Bison watched until he was out of sight,
then fell to the ground rolling and laughing, gradually becoming smaller
until nothing was left but a brown Coyote. "Oh, oh, ahh,
someone more pathetic than me. Oh, oh, I suppose I need
to get to the mountain ahead of him to give him the next set
of directions." But, then he saw a really cute shape in the distance
and hurried north. Screwed might have to wait until later
for his lesson—not a problem for the great Trickster.

The young man, unable to hunt, kept moving over the mountains, then
through the forest, then crossed a river.
In a cliff over the river, he smelled an old cave. Screwed stood
before the black hole in the rocks for a long time, because
he was afraid. Then, he carefully began to creep into the cave,
feeling his way in the darkness. His heart was beating like a drum
at a dance. Finally he saw a fire way back in the cave.
The shadows danced about the stone sides of the cave like ghosts;
and they frightened him. But looking, he saw on a ledge above
the far side of the fire, a great White Coyote, regal and aware
of him. With great fear in his heart, he knelt in front
of the fire respectfully and sang the song. At the end of the song,
the Coyote flowed down to him, stood and took the arrow
from him. "This arrow hit a Bison. Take it back

and you cannot miss your target. Take this with bow with it."

The young man bowed in gratitude. When he looked up, he saw an old man facing him, naked in the firelight, a face wrinkled with the seams of many years and trials, and framed by long white hair that the firelight played with. The eyes seemed yellow in that light.

"Smoke with me," said Old man, and passed the pipe to his visitor. After they had smoked, Old man said: "If you see me again, and I say that only the Great White Owl can change your luck, then shoot me with that arrow. Do not worry, do not change your name, do not fear luck. Things always change of their own course. Be well and go."

The young man left with gratitude for his gifts. The old man sat by the fire and took off his mask. Revealed, Mole smiled; she expected that when she saw Coyote again, he would have a fresh arrow in his butt. Thank the Spirit Coyote had never mentioned the Redoubtable White Woodlouse.

Coyote & the Rabbit Women

Coyote had been following the vision of a woman for days, when he came to a land ruled by rabbit women. He took the form of a handsome rabbit. He entered their village, leading with his majestic nose.

A little Rabbit ran up and hit Coyote in the balls with a Coup stick, which meant that Coyote belonged to his mother. He chased the rabbit into a teepee. Inside, many beautiful skins, decorated with quill and bead work, were hanging. The ravishing Rabbit woman left her cooking stew and shooed the boy outside.

The stew smelled good, but Coyote was 15,000 tastebuds short of a sophisticated rabbit tongue—on the other hand, her plump form filled his superior visual receptors.

Coyote reacted immediately and soon only an erection was holding up his leggings. He said, "I have swollen from the hit!"

Rabbit woman looked at it and said, "Is that all it is good for? Doesn't it get in the way when you run?"

Coyote looked confused, but then said, "No, it is for

connecting two bodies together."

"You mean like a needle? Do I have to poke it through my skin?"

"Sure," said Coyote, and placed his hand under her dress, "right here, and you will find it most agreeable."

He tenderly lowered her to a blanket and then jumped on her pumping wildly up and down, in and out. Then he said, "Roll over on your stomach and we can try another way." She groaned with pleasure.

Her mother and sisters heard and came into the tent. They wanted to see if it was as pleasurable for them, so they started taking off their dresses. But, Coyote's member had gone flat. Too many connections. But, the women all wanted to try it. He said, "Stop grabbing it," and he started being afraid. He said to the women, "I have to pass some water through this before it can charge up. I'll just stroll over to this hill. You can watch me."

When he got to the hill, he ran like crazy, dove into the Rio Rillito and floated away on a log. Perhaps this was too much of a good thing.

Uncle Rabbit Smokes a Briar

Coyote finally reached a warm sand bar and went to sleep. A while later, he woke up. He felt all his limbs with his eyes closed, just in case. He felt normal, opened his eyes, looked normal—for a rabbit, but what happened?

Having tricked Crow and Mink and Raven, as well as others, Coyote was intending to crown himself King of the Tricksters. The others could be his jesters when he held court. What could he add to that? Commissar of the Local Union of Tricksters, Entertainers & Musicians (LUTEMS)? Canis lutems. That sounded official.

Coyote was walking along the stream admiring his reflection, when he bumped into Rabbit, who dropped an empty sack. Coyote took notice and asked, "Why are you carrying a sack?"

Rabbit said, "This is to keep from being killed by hail stones this afternoon."

Coyote looked around, up at the sky, at his paws and noticed he did not have such a sack. "Could I have it?" he asked, "it would be tragic if I a commissar king were hurt by too much hail."

"No, but you could buy it with a fine shell," Rabbit suggested, throwing some pebbles into the leaves behind his back, and saying, "Uh, oh, could be hail coming."

Coyote opened his medicine bag quickly, and said, "Let me pay you for that, and you can make another for yourself."

Rabbit agreed and helped Coyote tie it on a low branch. Coyote got in it right away. Rabbit made noises for a while pretending to make another sack. Then, he shouted, "Oh, no, it's hailing, help."

Coyote smiled but did not come out of his bag to risk injury.

Then Rabbit threw pebbles and a few larger stones at Coyote's bag. The stones hurt and Coyote howled. Rabbit threw really big stones. One of the stones hit the tie and Coyote dropped to the ground.

Rabbit came up and said, "Are you all right? That was really violent!"

Coyote thanked Rabbit for saving him, "That was bad. Would have been worse without the bag." Rabbit left, then Coyote noticed the pattern of scattered stones and became suspicious. Coyote followed Rabbit.

When he caught up to Rabbit, he was sitting in front of an oblong paper ball hanging from the branch of a small tree.

"Did you throw stones at me?" Coyote asked.

"Not now," Rabbit said, "I am working. I was hired to finish teaching these children in here."

"I don't see any kids in there."

"They are napping, Listen, you can them humming in their sleep. If you give me another shell, you can finish teaching them and they will pay you for all the lessons. Wake them up in five minutes by hitting the ball with this stick. They have really poor hearing, so hit it really hard." And, Rabbit walked off.

Coyote waited 30 heartbeats then hit the hive so hard it broke in half and the Brazilian bees savagely stung him until he was swollen like a slug. Coyote was sure that Rabbit had tried to hurt him, so he was going to have to beat Rabbit severely, as soon as the swelling went down.

When he found Rabbit the next day, he was chewing on some pine gum. Coyote pointed to the red welts and demanded to know what was happening, why was Rabbit trying to hurt him?

Rabbit replied that he was making sunglasses to protect his eyes from the sun; everyone knew how dangerous the sun was now, hitting you with ultraviolet rays and neutrinos, damaging skin and eyes.

Coyote wanted the first pair immediately, and Rabbit agreed for a small price. Coyote was sure this, at least, was a good bargain. He knew his eyes turned red, dry and itchy from the glare on summer days.

Rabbit adjusted the sticky eye shields over Coyote's eyes.

"Hey, everything's a pretty yellow," said Coyote. "But I can see the sun."

Rabbit said, "Let me thicken them to protect you," and he added much more gum.

Coyote said, "Hey, it's too dark!"

"Don't worry," Rabbit said, "I'll make it lighter now."

Then he set fire to the dry grasses around Coyote, who ran off as the tree gum melted on his face and caught fire.

Coyote had to dive in the river to save himself. He was swollen worse and red and painful—oh, the pain of being a red man.

The next day, still swollen, red and patchy, bruised and stung, he followed the scent trail until he saw Rabbit tied loosely to a post like a scarecrow in a field of corn. Coyote could not help asking, "What happened to you? I don't care! You're trapped, you're mine now!"

Rabbit explained, "The farmer of this field hired me to scare off crows. He promised to pay me with a chicken and some corn at dusk."

"Oh, that is really stupid, you can't eat meat. Let me take your place and you can go back to eating lettuce," and Coyote loosed the knots and pulled Rabbit off the scarecrow stake.

Rabbit tied him tightly to the stake and reminded him of the cost of a chicken dinner, so Coyote gave him another shell.

When the farmer came to his field that evening, he saw
the frightening devil that had been stealing his chickens and corn
and blasted him several times with his shotgun. Then he dragged him
down to the river and threw him in. Funny, it didn't look quite like the
fox he remembered; it was red, but larger and lumpier, so it
must have been.

Coyote washed up on a sand spit and lay there ruined.
In the evening Fox came by for a drink of water before moving up
to the hen house for dinner. His intuition told him that the wretch
on the sand had been Coyote, but it looked like an angry mob had
beaten, burned and shot the poor bastard. Fox hesitated, then sighed,
and jumped over Coyote. Coyote stood up and said, "Are you going
hunting? I recommend Rabbit."
    "No, just up to a henhouse. Want to share a few clucks?"
        "No!" said Coyote, "Thanks, I'll just have some grass to
settle my stomach. You go on."
    Coyote watched as Fox went upstream, so Coyote went down
stream; that character always seemed to be around when he woke up.
What was that about?

Eyes in the Sky OR *Washed up at last*

Coyote was really hungry, then he found a patch of wild onions
and ate them. A few minutes later, he heard a gunshot
and was startled and jumped, but then it happened again
just behind him. He realized it was his own rear end firing.
Soon the sound of thunder from his own rear was pushing
him along the ground faster, then higher in the air.
He grabbed a tree to stay close to the ground. Finally, he fell
to the ground and buried his head in dirt. He knew
what he had to do. He found a white root and ate it.
But, that made him defecate until he was almost empty.
He had to climb back up the tree to avoid the mess.
Under his weight, the tree loosened its roots and fell over
a ravine. Coyote pooped several times into a hollow
and it ran out into the water. He fainted from weakness
and fell into the stream, which took him a way and washed him

up on the bank, unconscious.

When he woke, Coyote was too weak to waste time searching
for food. Then, he remembered hearing an idea of Spider's
and decided to throw his eyes into a tree. He took them out
and threw them into the top branches, saying the words,
'Hang there.' It worked! He could see the desert from the top of
the tree; there was a mouse 20 feet away. Excellent.
He called his eyes back, 'Drop to me,' but they didn't move.
Not good. He tried again but nothing happened. All he could see
was the low desert, so he tripped over the root of the tree.
"Who are you?" he asked.

"I'm the pine tree you gave your eyes to. I never realized
I was so isolated here."

Coyote asked, "Can you send them back down?"
The tree answered, "I don't know how. Besides they're useful
for looking for storms or birds."

Coyote cursed as he fumbled around on his knees.
Then he found some round tender globes and put them in his eye
sockets. They smelled like mushrooms, and he couldn't see
any better, although it did seem lighter. He had to get home
for help. He got up and started moving slowly, feeling his way.
He finally bumped into someone with his foot, "Who are you?"

"A cherry tree," spoke the tree with a slight pink soprano.
'Ah, I must be close to the stream,' Coyote deduced. He kept
moving and bumped into someone else, "Now, who are you?"

"Cottonwood," said a pleasing grey baritone.
"I must be really close to the stream," and he moved downhill
until he hit someone else. "Who the hell are you?"

"Willow," said a bright green contra-bass.
"I must be at the stream," Coyote said and he crawled until
he felt the water and fell into the stream. He drank as he drifted
with the current. He hit his head on a boulder and was washed up
on the bank. Two boys found him, and looking at his white
swollen eyes, realized he was dead.

"Is this coyote dead?" Jimjim asked.

"Yes, he smells bad," Benito judged. "Wait, let me rub
something, hmmm, he seems alive—at least part of him is standing."

They poked him for a while and then ran away to tell their friends so they too could come see the badly pulverized animal.

When Coyote woke up, he could smell food, wonderful rotting food, and a buzzing sound, but could not see anything.
"Who is that?" Coyote asked.
"Why, it's just us, the yellowjacket sisters, just looking for food," said one of the sisters, Nina, while the others, Tina, Mina and Gina, were eating a mouse from the inside.
Coyote crawled towards the smell. He reached out a paw and felt something, touching the leg of the mouse. Coyote asked, "What is that?"
They said, as one, "A stick."
Coyote felt around carefully and said, "It has eyes."
"It is a stick with eyes," the girls explained.
"It has paws, too."
"So, it is a stick with eyes and paws."
"And whiskers."
"Right, okay, a stick with whiskers, eyes, paws. What's unusual about that?"
Coyote fainted with hunger and weakness.
The yellowjacket sisters took pity on him and tied a bag under his tail, then put red lipstick on his lips, blue make-up on his eyes, and yellow tassels on his ears.
"Very pretty," said Tina. They rolled him into the stream and watched as he washed away. After a mile, Coyote floated by Trout, who thought to himself, 'Now, I have truly seen the Lady of the Lake.'
After another mile, Coyote got tangled in logs and drowned. Some days were like that, and there was a dead coyote on every beach, perhaps even the same Coyote.

Months passed and Coyote started to decompose after the birds and insects had their fill. After several more months, Fox trotted by and jumped over the bones and hairs. Coyote filled in and coughed. He was upset. He grilled Fox about his accidental proximity. Fox explained his instructions, but Coyote just shook his head and drifted downstream, confused and disoriented.

Coyote Loses Mole

Finally reunited with his saintly mate, whom he had tried to kill many times, when she refused to humor every whim, he was happy. They ate fresh mice, mated and slept in the den. Coyote woke up, but his mate did not. He shouted to her body—"Wake up! You were breathing yesterday! Remember!? Breathe!"

But, she, she could not; she had been taken by the Great Spirit. Coyote knew he could trick anyone and get her back.

He approached Spirit and asked, then begged and whined, until Spirit took pity on the mateless trickster, and told him what to do.

Coyote travelled west for five days to a great river. He put the end of his flute into the water and whistled. When he saw the canoe with two spirits in it, he averted his eyes, as instructed. He got in.

After they crossed Coyote leaped out to the shore. There were many houses, but no people in sight. Everything was as still as death. There was a very large underground house, so he went there. In it an old woman was sitting with her face to the wall; lying on the floor on the other side of the room was the moon. He sat down near the wall.

When the sun went down, hundreds of people began to enter, men, women, and children. Coyote saw Mole at last. When the room was filled, the old woman turned about, and jumped forward, five times, until she alighted in a small pit beside the moon. She raised and swallowed the moon, and it was pitch dark. The people wandered about, unable to see. At daylight the old woman then disgorged the moon, and laid it back in its place on the floor; all the people filed out. Coyote was alone.

He prepared for the next night. He hit the old woman on the head with a walking stick, then bound and gagged her, leaning her against the wall. Then, Coyote pretended to be the old woman, dressing in rags and speaking the same words of power. Soon, the people came in, and milled around like the night before. He was careful not to look at them or at Mole. He turned and jumped five times, trying to swallow the moon, unsuccessfully, then covering it barely with his hands. The people were quiet all night. When they streamed out at dawn, they entered a box he had made in front of the door, and they filled it. He swept leaves out the real opening and the leaves went where the people would have gone.

He left quickly. After a few hours, he placed his ear against it, and after a while distinguished the voice of his wife. He smiled. He travelled east, checking the sounds every night. On the fifth night, he opened the box to release his wife. The cover was thrown back violently! Dead people rushed into the air and disappeared in the west. He thought he saw the back of Mole's head as she rushed with them.

Coyote was devastated and returned to Great Spirit to beg for another chance. Great Spirit chastised him, "You see what you have done with your impatience and curiosity! If you had brought these dead all the way back, people would not die forever, but only for a season, like plants, whose leaves you scattered in place of the souls. Hereafter trees and grasses will die in the winter, and in the spring they will be green again, but people will die forever. You have made their deaths—all deaths—permanent."

"Let me catch them again," proposed Coyote.

"You cannot. They have gone where the moon is, in the sky," Great Spirit spoke and turned away from Coyote.

Coyote cried, "Why!? Why me!? Why her?" unable to connect the links between his acts.

Coyote could not think about it. He wandered to wintry lands, then to tropical ones. He had to eat, then sleep, for a few thousand years at least. No thoughts, no tricks … just be … still …

Coyote Returns

Coyote invents television Or Couch poetcheeto

Coming into the canyon surrounded by great rocks,
Coyote saw some children playing and figured
that they would want to play with him, but
he was wrong; they ignored him, and went on
running and hiding. Coyote thought, what kind
of game would they play with me, Coyote?

He went and found a cedar tree by the creek
and made a few beads out of its berries, colored
them with blue and yellow and put them on strings.
When he saw the children again, he waved those
beads and spoke to them; they paid no attention,
acted like he was some kind of adult.

Coyote did not like this; he needed to be noticed
and laughed at. He went to a distant village
and traded water to tobacco woman for tobacco
(he knew it will not rain and she could trade with
corn man). Back in the canyon that evening he made
a fire, waited for the careless children.

When he saw them, he lit his pipe and waved
it at the children, saying, "Look here, big fire, smoke,
great fun." But they continued their running game,
and as Coyote watched and smoked voluminously
his tail swept into the fire and ignited—he yipped
loudly knowing they must have smiled.

It was not enough. So, he traveled to a far distant village
of the people colored like ashes. He made a thing those
kids could never resist. He paid for help with promises
of fame, knowing the bargain was good (fame is
nothing). He put it in a mysterious box and carried
it for many weeks and for many miles.

Now at their own village, he tapped the current of
the earth, displayed the box at the edge of the well.
It was on when the children came out of their hogans
and they sat down beside the triumphant Coyote.
Then they all watched in silence together, as
the Roadrunner left Coyote in the dust . . .

Coyote steals a car Or Left in the dust

Hundreds of nights had passed, and Coyote lay
bathed in the gently flashing, funny light
of the magic box. Time for another snack
he thought and rolled over for corn chips.
No chips left; the children had gone he noticed,
tapping his belly with a dirty nail.

His belly trembled and kept shifting, then fell
to the side and raised a little dust. This is
odd, Coyote thought. How did this happen?
He stood and his belly bounced on the ground.
He fell over again and pushed it, poked
it, pressed it, played with it like a new toy.

The next day he went to see Gila monster,
who was lying on the sand in the sun,
thoughtfully tapping his own belly. "Look,"
Coyote said, and swung his belly over
his friend. In the shade, Gila nodded,
"What a fine belly, how can you carry it?"

Coyote flopped on his side, with his nose
near Gila's nose. Both exhaled for a while.
Coyote spoke slowly, "I cannot lose it, but
it is too heavy to carry very far—I will not
be able to chase any food or visit anyone."
Then Gila spoke, "why not get a car?"

They stood watching the highway. The cars
were too fast to catch, they agreed. "I know
where they nest," Gila said. That night,
Coyote couldn't decide, so many choices:
mustangs, vipers, pintos, jaguars, dusters,
then he saw it—the Plymouth *Roadrunner!*

Getting in was easy, the windows were open,
but turning the key—had to use his teeth.
Then he had to open the door for Gila
who said he knew how to do the things
on the floor to make it go. Then it did go,
a dark shape flying through the night.

Coyote grinned and howled with delight,
he pointed it down the darker ribbon, head
outside in the rushing air, Gila on the pedal
asking what was going by. Then Coyote saw
a mouse and turned the car to follow it.
The car bounced over two sandy ridges.

Gila was bounced off the pedal. The car stopped
in the sand. Gila got back on, but the wheels
only spun. After digging in a while, Gila left.
Listening to the engine rumble, Coyote howled
with frustration, then sighed, dialed for heat,
curled up in the seat and went to sleep.

Coyotes faces Godzilla Or *Yippi yi yi*

The car was too hot during the day, but gave
a nice shadow, so Coyote lay underneath it.
Having stolen a car, heck, having even stolen
the sun once, Coyote needed a new challenge,
but what? That would take a lot of thought.

So he thought, ate, thought, slept, thought,
thought, thought, ate, ate, slept, thought,
and the desert moved around him;
the cholla bloomed and the pear
but nothing bloomed in Coyote's head.

Too much work, he decided, best to eat
and sleep some more and see if ideas
would come when he wasn't looking
but the ideas were buzzing around
different heads elsewhere in the desert.

Coyote was irritated by the mouse
whose hole he was resting over
so he decided to teach the mouse
a lesson and eat him. He dug down
then to the right, then the left, and down.
Where was Badger when he needed help?

Mouse said, "Wait! What are you doing?"
"Just hanging around for dinner," said Coyote.
Mouse warned him, "Better not stay here,
the giant who kills everyone will see you."
"Oh, I'm not afraid of giants," Coyote boasted,
"why, I'll kill him if I see him. Fix his wagon."

"He's closer than you think, bigger than
you imagine," Mouse replied, "you might need
a really big stick." Coyote bared his teeth
and held up a paw, "See these," he said,

"these can cause pain in mice and men.
Look!" and Coyote danced the fighting dance
swinging wildly at shadows, hitting himself.
Mouse snuck off while Coyote was bragging.

Maybe Mouse was right, Coyote thought,
maybe there were beings with powers
greater than his. He saw a stick and picked
it up. He could hit him with this, finish
him before—where was the mouse?

But the Mouse was watching from
the saguaro on the hill, having left
through the back door. Coyote was
still five feet from the door and looking
dusty and hot. He snuffed at the dirt.

It was getting hotter, but then a good
cloud made shade and he started
digging again. Part of the cloud
pointed at the mountains. No, the shade
was from a mountain. Coyote looked up

and saw a giant Gila monster, something
too big, too unnatural—Coyote dropped
his stick, yipping pathetically, tail tucked,
he blazed a trail east, not looking back;
maybe it was just a bizarre shadow
cast by a mouse, but maybe it was better
to come back and find out later . . .

Coyotes goes nuclear Or *Thatsa one spicy meataball*

The shadow had scared him he could admit;
he was quivering like an agave worm,
even if he was not sure what it was
exactly, a Gila monster larger than oak trees
larger than boulders and even some mountains.
If it came back, he had to have protection,
something that guaranteed his security
that is, if it wasn't his imagination.
What could hurt it? Large teeth or claws?
He had seen machines tear the earth with claws
large enough; he had to think. He slept.

It was cold again all night, he shivered.
Coyote had burrowed in the ground, but he got dirty;
he had used fire before and danced around it,
but that was too much work, all that wood gathering,
bending over, poking, getting more wood, feeding
the flames. There had to be a better way.

He had seen the planes go over, these metal birds
of men, pushed by glowing branches,
carrying strange things from town
to town. He remembered where one had gone down
and burrowed in; and he could go there on his own
without the dance of badges and papers.

In a remote part of the desert, he found it,
half-buried. He dragged a long tube from the sand,
dragged it through the desert, for nights, then
buried it by a mesquite, next to den number 63.
It kept the den warm at night. Night after night
it was hot, and he could not get too close, so
he buried a bit away, behind a wall of sand.
He was warm, but then some fur and teeth started
to fall out. Must be getting old he thought,
have to find a woman, make a boy to carry on
the sacred traditions of being Coyote.

Coyote reproduces

Coyote takes a mate Or Learning to wait

Coyote was running around one day, he ran
around from place to place, rock to tree, mesquite
to prickly pear, rubbing off his scraggly mangy painful
fur. Under the greasewood, he sat too tired
to move but itching.
                    "You need help," he heard
a voice say. He looked up and saw Mountain Lion.
draped across a limb. "What happened?" Lion asked.
      "I must be too hot." Coyote answered, "but water
doesn't help; soon, I'll be furless. Could you scratch
this?" he asked.
                    "No, I don't think so," Lion purred,
"but you could get a mate."
                          'A mate' thought Coyote, rolling
over, that would solve everything. "Where would I start?"
            "Talk to Flicker," answered Lion, "he is always
nosing around into everyone else's business."

Coyote knew there were females around. He had seen them
looking at him when he hunted and he watched
them back. "But watching won't get you a mate,"
Flicker said, "you need to woo a woman, make
her feel special, then pin her to the sand. For a special price,
I will set up a date and provide flowers and sweet meats."
                "Okay," said Coyote, "I'm game."
            "Exactly," said Flicker, "sign here, initial here, piss there."

Standing in front of the clean new den, Coyote
was disgruntled: Play the field, ha; all he had gotten
was dirty. Have parties, ha; all he had gotten was used
for entertainment. The voluptuous Mink said that she
would mate with him, but had to have her own
den. Jacqueline Rabbit said she would mate with him
but she had to have willow twigs to eat every day.
Ducky ignored him. He needed to try a new approach.
So he asked Kingfisher for help. Kingfisher said he knew

of a young female who lived by the flat mountain;
he would make arrangements. He did. On the right day
Coyote saw her by the streambed. She did not run away;
she stood by her prize, a mouse, backed up when
he approached and let him eat it. After several more,
he asked 'why,' since he was older and slightly mangy.
She Wakanda said she heard that he was a great explorer
(and thought he could be reformed into a good provider).
He renamed her Coyota, thought she would be a good
provider, and suggested that they hunt that night together.
They hunted together well, and traded fluids.
They decided to make a new den by the hill.
And his fur started growing back, although
he remembered the glowing metal longingly;
but she would not hear of them living near it.

She wanted to get married, let some family and friends
see how happy they were. "I'll do all the work," she urged
and that was that. Soon the presents started arriving:
road runner traps, how-to-cook books—not funny,
those—even a cottonwood penis extender, which
disappeared immediately, and mice, many dead mice.

The ceremony was the very epitome of dignity,
promises were made, lies were exchanged, the bride
was dusted white, the groom's tail resined black.
Favors were traded for the banquet. The best animal
Raven forgot the ring, the maid of honor Badgera
went topless, and the minister was drunk on berries.
Blackbird caught the bouquet and flew off.

Somehow they got back to the den. Coyote announced:
"Time for wedding night coyitus! It is the coynage
of the realm, coystyle!" He really wanted
to mate like a wolf, but couldn't get turned around
properly. Wakanda didn't want her dust smudged, just
yet, so they lay back and barked at the moon,
yipped and barked, barked and yipped until
the sun rose and they sank into sleep.

Getting analyzed Or *Picked apart by Vulture*

For weeks Coyote lay in the den, depressed. He no longer
admired his stomach, which had gotten bigger, no longer lusted
to speed through the night, was jittery about large shadows
from strangely shaped clouds, and was always playing with a bald
patch near his tail that never grew back. He never wanted to
mate, complained Wakanda, "Is it because I am fat with pups,
your pups? And, my name is Wakanda, not Coyota! I'm not one
of your appendages, buster!"

Coyote groaned, more responsibility was looming.

Wakanda told him there must be something wrong;
he should be happy, now. Although he acted dignified
yet slinky sometimes, she was embarrassed to be with him
in front of her friends. He needed to see a specialist,
get better fast, maybe Desert Insurance would cover it.

So they went to see Doctor Vulture, beneath the topless
yucca tree. "You know," the Doctor said, "I have helped
others worse than you—eagle for instance, who used
to skulk around eating dead cows—now look at him,
national symbol and all. Then there was Badger, soon to
represent a football team—"

"What about Rattlesnake?"
Wakanda interrupted.

"Ah, that is a sad story, but with more
time, deeper analysis—but we want to help you now, if
you want to change."

"He does," said Wakanda.

"Well, let's begin,
eh?" Doctor Vulture leaned over Coyote, "do you love your
mother? Who was she?"

"The moon of course," Coyote said,
"How could anyone get warmth from the moon?"

"Your father?" Vulture continued.

"Myth, hardly knew him, he sprayed and ran."
The session went for days, Wakanda bringing them mice, water.

After a functional analysis of Coyote (Inputs: air, water, food,
dirt. Needs: warmth, others, victims. Outputs: saliva,
spunk, excrement), Doctor Vulture said it was common
treatable dual personality bipolar disorder. "Think," he said,
"you are revered as creator, great hunter, sacred supervisor,
and yet," Doctor Vulture paused, "hated as coward and thief.
This negative image is behavioral: From darting away at the first
sign of trouble to eating other animals, well, eating anything."

Coyotes muscles tensed to run, but Wakanda leaned
on his foot.

"You are burdened with the reputation of a greedy
bungler, easily duped by children or slow animals."

"But wise enough to howl
at the approach of the unknown," Coyote added.

"Hmm," said the Doctor, "you know, I rarely
give specific advice, but new ages require new sages, so
here goes: Act your age, you're about to be a father now
and cannot go trying to change your colors like bluebirds
or lizards. Don't get into trouble, think about your mate.
Ignore all the things you cannot change, move more slowly.
Give up your old sneaky friends like Raven and Snake, find
other couples with children. I would recommend that you get
the tail cropped and learn to stand and point, like a dog,
so that people will see your natural dignity. Gain a little
weight, like that stomach; and don't ever show your teeth."

Coyote lay where he was, slowly lifted his tail and let it flow
down again; it didn't raise any dust. This is it, he thought, the end
of exploration and excitement, the end of life.

Wakanda nipped his tail and said, "You can laugh, and
things will flow and change themselves."

Coyote yipped and laughed, 'ah, well, what else?'

Then Wakanda called him to dinner: Fruit from saguaro
and organ pipe cactus, like watermelon, a stinkbeetle
and blotched-lizard, with grasshopper mouse for desert.

Four pups were born. 'That was easy' thought Coyote, and he let
Wakanda name them. He felt a little useless, but free.

Coyote steals ice cream Or Supermarketing city dog

Coyote was sensitive, oh so sensitive; he watched jets
cross the sky and was interrupted by a distant ambulance,
then a Stinkbeetle crossed the path that could not not
be nosed and followed, licked and teased, tasted—
"*ucchh, cacchhh!*" —and spit out. Coyote was hungry, now.
And, he knew where he wanted to go out to eat.

He was a city dog, now, city dog, loping through Tucson,
and that was Packrat's fault for saying there would be food
and adventure, so many new things and tastes. But so
much hard black sand everywhere in ribbons and squares
and hard noises. He rolled in the black stuff to blend in, lifted
his leg by giant strangely shaped stones and pissed frugally.
From a shadow of a square mountain in a straight
canyon, he lifted his nose to taste the sweat of people
moving between their freezing inside-up and out dens
and their moving freezing dens, all those colored metal
hard freezing rolling dens like the one he stole—

Never did get it out of the sand pit it dug itself in; never
did get Gila monster to admit it was his fault. Dug in,
dugs. He missed Wakanda. Maybe he should have brought
the pups, maybe next time, or send the pups to Uncle
Mickey's den and take Wakanda hunting for gourmet city
mountain mice. God, he was hungry. Dugs he was thinking,
too, and lifted tails and shared saliva on food, saliva,
so much, ahh. He could smell the scents of many females,
but they were mostly the silly frenzied females that
accompanied the silly humans in their march
from freezing dens to freezing foods—

Food! Humans! All he had to do was find a hungry one
and follow her. Confidently he moved from the hills
to the center, yard by desert yard, then park by grassy
park, until he was near a spindly metal tree
with human markings (Speedway) and the smells

were overwhelming. From a smaller shadow he could see
food behind transparent walls portioned out by smaller
humans, betas to the larger alphas, no doubt. No way
for him to fit in there. Back on a quiet smaller trail
he mused, then sneezed because he smelled
so artificial, then inspected the square above the dens
from under trees.
                        He saw evidence of other coyotes
near old food sites, once a mat of concentrated
excreted cat fur. At last, a human walking, and with
a silly retarded dog and an empty external pouch.
He stayed a short chase back and was rewarded soon,
but then the dog was tied in front and the female
went inside. Like mice, humans had three openings
to their food dens, but all were in plain sight, how odd,
what was the purpose of that? The silly bitch saw him
and started barking, such ignorant phrasing. Coyote
remembered the lessons of Doctor Vulture, raised his tail
and pranced through the far opening as gates of clear sand
parted and the air turned cold. The smells were strangely
muted; there on one path was the female with a small
hard den on wheels, but she had to push it—
perhaps Gila monster had broken it too. Then he saw
squares of grass, then piles of fruits, then rows of meats.

He paused, but then heard a loud threatening bawl.
A large male in white artificial smooth fur bore down
on him with complex barking, so Coyote raced
for the meats. He turned to throw off pursuit,
going down another trail with strange useless things,
but startled a female, who dropped a box. He flipped
it into his mouth and it froze to his lip. He stopped
and banged it on the path, then put his paw on it,
then his paw was stuck. He started to run, but the frozen
thing faintly smelling like milk but icy, hit the ground
first with each right front step, causing a lumpy gait
and slowing him. Finally he shed its icy embrace
and he could run. Now three males were chasing him.

His tail hit a pile of soft denning material with special
markings (toilet tissue), knocking them on the path.
Too many humans, he decided and slide through another
pile of food (doughnuts), missing a bite, then raced
past the funny gates, mouthing a last prize (onion rings)
from a high black moving path, and down to the outside.
The female mutt was still barking; she slipped her neck rope
and chased him down the large busy trail. Maybe
she wanted to mate, and he should let her catch him.

No, it wasn't mating, or taking the strange greasy
vegetable matter from him. She sat away from him,
she sat a distance from where he lay, not barking
any more, near a herd of fast metal dens, cars
he had heard them called. He tried to convince
her to help him take one but she was stupid
and misunderstood how to make them go—
probably thought Coyote wanted to mate in one,
like humans. He stood and she jumped and retreated,
barking. 'Great, my personal alarm,' he thought. He loped
off, determined to find a smaller food den; she stayed.
He turned back, thinking that he should try to make
her wild, spark that small flame of wildness
that every animal, even domestic ones, had. Then
his nose led him to a giant multiple den (Cortez mall),
with a vast herd of moving dens on one wide black path.
He circled it, counting the humans and decided
to prudently give up that one, too much trouble.

He continued east towards the desert; private
den areas became larger and travel was easier, despite
the dogs everywhere. Then, he smelled other animals.
He crept over a small hill. Many were there, in impossibly
small territories, but with much food. He had heard of this
once. Perhaps it was the heaven where food came
to you? He could not find coyote territory, maybe
there were none here—but he found wolves.
They did not bark, but he read their murderous

curious eyes. He moved on. Deer, but no mouse
areas. What kind of place was this? It had a marking
tree (Zoo). No dog areas either, but a Gila monster
and Vultures. He asked the Vultures for food; and,
they refused, not knowing him or not caring.
Were they ignorant or rudely spoiled by heaven?
He had to rest, so he found a tree and slept beneath it.

Lying under a scrawny ironwood, he thought he could trade
for food, or invent a thing to make food, but he needed
food to think, then he saw a human pup holding
food. He was plump, so he must be addicted to cheese balls
and television, 'ah, those days,' Coyote remembered fondly.
The pup too had mangy sparse fur, so he must have hot
metal in his den for warmth; Coyote unconsciously rubbed
the patch near his tail. The pup was holding a cold
milk lump—were there no cheetos at all in this city?
The male pup saw him and spoke, "nice doggy," the insult
rolling off Coyote like a milk lump off a hot tongue. Coyote
lowered his head and wagged his tail and as the pup went
"ewwww" when he petted Coyote's oily black patch
disguise, Coyote snuffed the lump into his mouth
and ran. The pup screamed and rubbed his hands
on his white smooth fur, dancing the human anger dance.

Success, Coyote thought as he raced to a copse of oaks
overlooking a pond with many pink, long-legged birds.
He swallowed the lump and immediately had an aching
head; he licked the inside of his mouth and the milk
tasted better; the pain diminished. He looked at the birds
and wondered about their taste. He lay down and licked
some grass. A successful forage, he wondered if he should
bring some back. No, better not. He thought of all
the things he had stolen. He made a list of all the things
he had stolen in his life: The sun, fire, life, a maiden's virtue
and her son at the coast, immortality, the blueness
of bluebirds, the brownness of dust (well, that was
a mistake actually, after he tripped, damn it), cars, nuclear

warheads, and now, lumpy cold milk (ice cream).
What was next? Chocolate cake? An open multi-roomed
den mall? There was no limit to his ambition. Satisfied
that he had not lost any skills, he slept contentedly.

Wakened suddenly by cold water hitting him, he saw
a man with a mechanical snake spitting pure cold water
and he ran for the desert. But, then nearby, he found
objects full of old unfinished food. He had heard
of these sacred manna garbage mountains. He gorged
on the wealth. When his stomach bounced on the sand,
he pronounced it good and left. He would recount
this to Wakanda and the pups, the tales to tell as their fat
little bodies wormed next to his majestic big body,
Wakanda proud and waiting for his attention, too.
He walked on, following the vapor trail home.

Coyote plays dead

At first it was fun, the pups worshiped him, they gave
him their total attention, and he taught them to be
coyotes: When to yip, when to run, when to fight
(if your opponent was smaller and weaker), how
to find food, how to catch it (a decent five percent
of the time, although Wakanda seemed to always near
thirty, bitch), how to keep it by not sharing—
he refused to vomit it back when they licked
the corner of his mouth—they needed to learn
dignity and self-reliance, too; even humans knew—

Then the dung and mucus, the barking and crying,
the lessons, the sheer responsibility of fatherhood
began to wear on him. He spent more and more
time with Badger and Rattler, playing games
of chance and losing his food. He searched
elsewhere for attention. Wakanda, once Coyota, spent time
with the girls, Skunka and Eagla, comparing recipes
and fur (or feather) patterns, the slatterns. The pups
were getting big enough to shake their toes after
they pissed on them. He felt less needed, unheeded,
depleted and unseated as master of his den, so
when should he leave and where should he go?
He needed to be appreciated, he wanted to be needed,
he needed a new challenge. He could help other
animals cope with the uncertainties of desert life,
the certainties of human encroachment on their
fair desert sandscape. That was it. He would do that,
he would, yes, he would; the Hollywood Arizona
desert community would have a new name, new
purpose, new error, er, era of prosperity, and he
would be the looter, la, leader—

Then the pups jumped him and he played dead.
"Dad," they said, "tell us another story."
                                        He rolled

so his ribs sprang back and said, "We're going
to throw our spit in the ring. Play the politics game.
Denny, you get flyers—"

          "What are flyers, dad?"

  "Talking birds, you get them. Spotty, go get Badger.
Humpy, think about a campaign slogan—"

    "It's Humphrey, Dad, and he's Spotsworth."

   "—or a good lie, whatever. And, Renren, stay between your
mother and me. C'mon, no more messing around. It's time to
seek power over the peasants. Let's go!"

Running for Mayor Or Promising a pound of flesh

Coyote said it was time to let Eagle retire, his ideas
were stale, his leadership weak. Animals were starving,
humans were racing around in mobile dens, killing
animal people and kidnapping cacti. Coyote offered
to feed all the animals and to protect the cacti.

The community met in the bottomland by the stream,
so all could drink peacefully while they talked, except
that Rattler swallowed a mouse before they began;
they made him cough her up and warm her until she
could breathe again. Rattler apologized with a hiss.

Peccary and Turtle wanted to run against Coyote. Eagle
saw the writing on the sand and withdrew as a lame
duck leader; he had ambitions beyond the stream anyway.
Each candidate was to give a speech and then the community
would vote. Coyote started, the pups interrupting him
with cheers and howls.
        Coyote said, "My platform is food for everyone."
If animals could not get enough food, he Coyote
would give each a mouse, except the mice,
who would each get a mushroom, that is, if
there were enough mice left to be hungry. Mouse
spoke up and said that Misses Mouse assured him
that they would outnumber everybody by next month
and could swing the election for some seeds and fungus.
Coyote coughed to cover up his swallowing Misses
Mouse whole, winking at Rattler. Then, Dung-beetle
spoke, saying that he could not use a mouse, but
sometimes more dung. And Bat spoke, saying
that he only ate mosquitoes. Coyote promised one
mosquito to each bat, but Bat replied that mosquitoes
were much lighter than mice, so he would need 97
mosquitoes a day. Coyote promised 98, but no one
thought he would ever catch enough for one bat,
much less the 6548 bats in the community. Coyote

was weak on math, about like a creosote bush.
The mosquitoes wanted a guarantee of two animals per night
to suck on; would Coyote be one? Coyote smiled weakly
and nodded. Wakanda boffed his head sideways.

Peccary presented his platform, which was strangely
porcicentric. He spoke directly to the large animals—
wolf, cougar, bobcat, deer, and wolverine—suggesting
that humans were too good at hunting. To make
things more fair, he suggested making winter colder
or longer, with desert snow. All the large animals
agreed. Wolf suggested asking the small animals too
so when they asked great spirit, who made us, for approval,
they would have a stronger position.
                                        Coyote sniffed
loudly, "He hasn't made anything easy for us lately,"
thinking 'I, Coyote, am a god. Did we suddenly forget that?'
     But the other animals ignored him. So, they asked
opinions from Porcupine, Beaver, Mouse, Raccoon,
Martin, Bobcat, Jackrabbit, Frog, Turtle, Bat, Beetle, Mosquito,
Wren, Bee, Wasp, and some of the lesser, hard-to-see
or even hear insects.
                                        Peccary repeated his strategy.
The large animals agreed, but the small were silent.
     Finally Turtle spoke: "That's good for you since you
have fur and fat, but we and the insects will get cold
and not be able to get food."
                                        The large animals
liked Peccary's argument and wanted to go ahead, but
then Turtle asked a pointed question: "If it is that cold,
and the berries freeze and plants die, won't you starve
in the spring? Of course, we small ones should survive because
we can eat bark and grubs underground." He banged
his head on his shell to show how serious he was.
The large animals were speechless.
                                        Peccary admitted
that it made sense. He agreed to alter his promise
to limit cold weather to three months.

Now Turtle spoke his words slowly, and in fact many
of the animals entered a state not unlike sleep. Turtle
said he could not promise food for everyone, that
he could not change the weather, but he could
use common sense so that things were more balanced
in the whole desert ecosystem. He suggested sending
a group of representatives to Defenders and Greenpeace
to keep the mobile things, called 'bikes' or 'orvs,' away
from their homes. They would stress the value
of a clean healthy desert and the importance of all
the animals in the scheme of things. He suggested
allowing the status quo of eating and mating to continue
as it had in the past. Wolf hurrahed and thought
that they might take back some territory from the coyotes.
Turtle said he would appoint Peccary first as Vice
Mayor and include insects and mice on the City Council.
Coyote was so shocked he coughed up Misses Mouse, again,
who shook off the saliva and went off with Mister Mouse.
The community was pleased with the words of Turtle
and elected him as their Mayor.

Turtle said, "So it shall be: No pie-in-the-sky food
subsidies, no extended seasons. The animals can
go to their homes and the plants remain standing
or crawling." As Turtle walked by Coyote, he accidentally
butted him with his hard shell and stepped on
Coyote's tender pads with his nailed toes. Coyote yipped,
and Turtle said to the community, "How could you trust
someone who promises too much and then yips
at the slightest inconvenience."
                    Wakanda had to lead
Coyote off before he tried to turn Turtle over and start
to eat his sweet meats. Coyote even growled
at Porcupine and Mosquito, but stepped on his own
tail and yipped. Things had gone well, he thought,
suggesting a re-election strategy to her.

Hunting a mouse Or *Vacating mouseland*

How did turtle get elected? What a shock. The hard-nosed
bastard bought the votes, that's how! The animals chose
the political hack who promised them food and not
the pure candidate who offered them equality and dignity,
the dignity of Coyoteness! And now, exile beckoned.
Scat, how could it turn so bad so quickly?

"Road trip," Wakanda suggested.
                                    Coyote started immediately,
but the family followed and never let him out of their sight.
     "Are you going west?" she asked, blinded by the evening
sun. Coyote did not know where he was going, maybe
to the western waters. Several cycles of light passed
and they still kept moving. There were always mice,
or garbage. The pups were almost full-grown, with greasy
fur and burping oily bubbles—perhaps less garbage
and more mice, Coyote thought, burping himself,

Then he heard the sound of water on rocks, the rhythm
of water. Coyote came to a small mound of sand.
Beyond it, great waters washed in as swells
and crashed onto sands of broken shells. 'Careful,'
the cowardly muse in his head said, 'this is an unfamiliar
place, scary but exhilarating.' Coyote reminded himself
of the safety of his lair, security with Wakanda
and his pups, his support—and lush tropical meats—
Coyote remembered that exploring could lead to feasting.
He found a path to the beach, looked around, no dogs,
no humans. Funny birds with thin legs or giant sagging
cheeks. He motioned for his mate and pups to come over
the dune. Renren tripped and buried his nose in the sand,
legs splayed. Coyote rolled his eyes. Who had inherited
his grace? He sniffed the air for dead flesh. Smells
permeated his snout and senses; Salt air, fish, seaweed,
dead inedibles; he stepped in a tidepool and checked
it out; worms, crabs, anemone, spiky urchin, sea-stars—

58

"ouch!" he yipped with surprise, stepping on one.

Sunset, then nightfall, were consistent anyway.
They were all tired and hungry from trying to eat
sharp irritating things. Their paws sunk deep into sand;
muscles hurt. *"Argh!"* cried Coyote, not the right
environment, not the right time. They found
some softer grasses back on the second dune
and slept til dawn. Their ears hurt from the unrelenting
waves and the almost constant chattering of gulls.
Coyote had to compete for breakfast with the pups
at a trash can. Just as he spotted a half sour-creme donut
and bent to scarf it up, a gull plucked it from him,
the precision flight perfectly executed between the teeth
and the donut on the sand. Coyote howled in frustration.
but even his admiration for the skill of the theft
could not overcome his basic irritation.

They trekked inland, paralleling the black trails, expressways
to anywhere, the metal dens so fast, they could get hurt.
No place to hide, he sensed danger. Suddenly Denny
followed a scent. The metal tree sign said "truck stop."
A large mobile den had markings: "Fulks Run Chicken Farm."
There were hundreds of squawking chickens in cages.
Coyote jumped aboard, through a swinging door in back
of the rig in front of the trailer. He urged the family
to hitch a ride. They curled up in an old blanket, thick
with dog smell. The chickens were aware of his presence
and squawked louder; then, a human shouted he would put
his foot up their asses if he heard any more squawking.
One of the pups started to howl, but Coyote cuffed
him and his mate cuffed him smartly. Coyote could not stop
salivating, but holed metal separated them from the objects
of their desire. There was no way to eat one. They took
naps, whimpering dreams of bird flesh. Then took more
naps, then woke up to changes in movement.

The truck followed an exit sign that had the marks for mouse

land. It was lunch time. There was a picture of giant mouse.
Wakanda said it was the giant picture of a small mouse, but
they should go now, chickenless, and explore the possibilities.
At the next stop, they ran with wild abandon back
to the entrance gate.

"Oh, look mommy," said a human pup,
"see the cute doggies, I want to pet them."

"Don't touch
them, dear, just poor strays with mange," she replied.
'Bitch,' Coyote thought and snuck a snout under her skirt,
pleased when she shrieked and jumped at the cold noser.

The pups found the garbage area. "I'll have some
of that, and that, and that, and that, and—" said Denny.
Coyote found culinary treasure and gorged; his stomach
bulging, he got on a chair on a large wheel to take a
rest. But it started moving and headed for the sky. It swung
and Coyote vomited. Fortunately, it was good and could
be licked up later. He looked over the side; the people below
did not seem to be enjoying their share.

Wakanda climbed on a padded
box—it suddenly went up a steep hill and roared down—
she jumped off, vowing never again to get on that dizzy thing.
Denny and the pups dragged a can into the shrubbery
and kept recycling the food.

Finally Coyote got off the wheel
and found a quiet place to hide, but it was taken by a dirty
old human, who introduced herself, as if Coyote could
understand.

"Hi, I'm Babe Martin, my friends call me Psychobabe.
What is your name?"

Coyote looked for a place to lay.
"Are you Coyote the trickster of mythical stature? I'll share
the blanket, but I was here first. What's wrong with that tail?"

Coyote burped and left, looking for better grass.

Coyote had never seen a place where everything moved
and where some humans pretended to be animals and others

hid in shrubbery. Then he heard a commanding bark:
"Hey you!"

"What me, Coyote?"

"*Freeze!*"

Coyote froze mid-stride.
"Come here, you scroungy dog! You have to be leashed
and accompanied by your master at all times!"

A large human beast wearing a blue uniform with a wide belt
displaying a dizzying variety of tools and toys, gun, knife,
whistle, beeper, stick, phone, and other black leather secrets,
collared and leashed Coyote and took him to the Mouseland
Security Office for investigation and containment.

'Busted,' sighed Coyote, 'Wakanda will punish
me for this. Time to be a friendly pooch,' Coyote thought,
remove intelligence from the eyes, release the tongue,
and arch the back and tail.

The guard seized Coyote by
the scruff, forced a muzzle over his snout and cuffed
the front paws.

The other guard in the office, filing reports,
could not believe it, "What are you doing, it's just a dog;
take that off and take him to the pound for the owners
to pick up."

The first guard answered: "Are you kidding,
look at this guy's eyes. He's planning something or my name
ain't Pat O'Rooney." Addressing Coyote directly, he said:
"Okay, lets see now, how did you get in here? Can't
you read? No pets or animals allowed!"

Coyote only
looked at the guard, drooled and nosed at the posters
of Mickey, Minnie, Goofy, Porky, Daffy, and Pluto,
at the forms of the stuffed animals on the shelves,
doubtless dropped by tourists who had too many
to count.

"Oh, wise guy, eh?" the guard said. "Back
to the questioning: Who are you? Don't see any ID
tags on you. Where is your owner?" Coyote's gaze
returned to contemplation of the size of those perfect mice,

drooling saliva on the desk. It was mythic to have such heroic
rodents.

As if reading his mind, the guard said:
"No, you mangy stray, it's a just theme park for humans
to enjoy the anthropomorphic absurdity of giant peaceful
animals. The little kiddies love it, the adults feel young
again, and the place makes tons of money for some foreign
investors. Now let's get down to business, shall we?"

"I've been watching you, getting ready. I am charging
you formally with the following offenses: Attacking
Chuck Persinger, the dizney mouse, and ripping the back
of his costume, for which he or you will have to pay;
urinating on a fire hydrant (there were no rooms with pictures
of Coyotes on the doors, Coyote thought); audibly growling
during a parade spectacular on Main Street, scaring two little
children who are used to animals speaking in high whiney
voices (one of them had pulled my tail first, Coyote thought);
stealing a corn dog from little girl (actually saved it from falling);
overturning a popcorn cart (well, it exploded first);
taking cotton candy from little boy (Coyote shrugged);
frightening the trainer at bird show (who frightened the birds
first, then bribed them to act unnaturally); defecating
on a canoe on a Pirates of the Caribbean ride; masquerading
as a dog actor in the pantomime show, showing your penis
to the audience (Coyote smiled); sneaking on a roller
coaster without paying; eating hamburgers off the griddle;
lapping water from the rock fountain, and of course,
being unaccompanied and unleashed. Shall I go on?
Hmmm? So, you think your pretty clever coming in here
and causing trouble. Well, do you have anything to say
for yourself?"

Coyote shuddered for a moment, then
with feeling whined rhapsodically several of the dizney
tunes he had been hearing all day. Starting with: "When
you fish upon a star, makes no difference what they are—"

A tear rolled down the guard's cheek. He rubbed Coyote
on his head, and said, "Oh, go on, get outta here ya silly

dog. I can't be mad at you, but I have to take you outside
so you can wait for your family in the parking lot."

Coyote raised his forepaw in gesture of peace with the other
heavy beast, and heaving a heavy sigh, abdomen bloated,
tongue dangling, saliva dripping, pocketed a box of acme
explosives, and licked the hand that escorted him through
the exit turnstile.

He passed a strange thin character in black
and looked into the eyes of Death.

The figure smiled at him
and whispered, "Another immortal I see," and something
about being a trickster himself, then touched Coyote
on the hip by the tail, curing his mangy patch.

Coyote coughed
up a piece of plastic wrapper, nodded and strolled on.
Imagine that, he thought, Death on vacation. Where was Fox,
in case he needed him? He should have warned Death
to stay away from the cotton candy and chili.

It was only an hour wait until the family joined him
in the parking lot. Wakanda was carrying Spotty in her mouth
and laid him on the sand by the asphalt, not speaking.
Spotty had eaten too much; he lay still, not breathing.
"*Breathe!*" shouted Coyote, "you were just breathing this morning.
Have you forgotten already?" and he pushed on Spotty's
chest but no breath came out.

Wakanda was beside herself.
She demanded: "Bring him back! **Now!**"

"No, death is permanent
now. I cannot get him back."

"Try. Again. For *me!*"

Coyote left
without a word. He had an idea. He went to the surveillance
office, with a disheveled Bill Gates mask, and asked to see the
video records of people in the park. After hours of watching,
found Spotty on the tape. He asked the guard where the images
were stored now. The guard said, "in the computer."

Coyote said: "I know that.

I don't have to be told."

The guard said Coyote could access the mainframe from the station.

Coyote said," I am aware of that. I invented these things, after television. I can go in and get him back." But he couldn't get him back. All he could do was watch the record of Spotty. Time for a trance journey, he thought, into the hyperworld of silicon and silliness. The image could be made flesh, the data reincorporated, but first he decided to play a few games of Doom, killing off great numbers of goons and soldiers. Somewhere he accidentally erased Spotty and made haste to get back to the lot. Wakanda and the pups were quiet, knowing he had strained mightily to bring their brother back to life. He slunk towards them, as Wakanda started to howl in mourning.

Perhaps it was time to get back to the desert, where real people outnumbered humans. He howled as they walked to the freeway; an alligator came out of the side ditch and looked at the reduced Coyotes for a while. The Coyotes looked at the alligator. Neither thought the other would be easy food. Eventually, some third-generation hippies in a flatbed truck, with two German shepherds with macramé collars, picked up the Coyote family and drove them back east towards the desert, only a day's ride in the truck.

Three weeks later, he rolled over in the dirt, his dirt, and looked around. The canyon was quiet. Even the pups were sleeping; some ants disappeared under the brown tail of Renren, the runt. He suddenly howled, waking up the pups and their mother. She looked at him sternly and reminded him "Remember what Doctor Vulture told us, move slowly with quiet dignity, give up your noisy troublesome ways."

Coyote answered: "Wasn't me. But it is who I am, I pace, worry, yip, act out, nervous personality and all. Coyotes are the most sensitive, expressive animals alive. We cannot help ourselves."

She nodded, in the way that some understanding women do, and said, "Oh, go on, dance and sing, but do it quieter, where neighbors don't always see you." Then she added. "You are the alpha leader, and others depend on you."

Coyote looked at his mate, "You know I have no regrets. Perhaps we could find some succulent meats to share this evening, if you would like?" She raced ahead of him.

Interludes

Coyote in the bag

Coyote was hungry. He had nothing left but his wits
and an empty bag. He had an idea. He threw in a few sticks
and blew in the bag. He went to where the Cactus mice
were playing. "What's in the bag, Coyotlbozho?" one small
mouse asked.

        "Songs, for dancing, but I can't reach them.
Can a few of you help me and carry them out?"

      When five went in Coyote snapped the bag shut and ran
off. But then he heard singing from the bag. (One of the mice
was singing to cover up the sound of the others chewing.)
Coyote put the bag down; he struggled to untie the knot, then
looked up. He snuffed the recent scent.

    Rattlesnake had smelled the scent also and came to the bag,
going in the hole. The mice snuck up and closed the hole.
The small one said "Coyotlyodel, we changed our minds
and came back for another song."

        Coyote was puzzled,
since he knew there were no songs in the bag, but
he stuck his head in—

Coyote partnership stink

"Skunk, I need you to help me with a food problem. You like
mice?" Coyote whispered the plan in his ear.

    Skunk slunk back to his underground house and lay down.
Coyote raced to the Mouse area and shouted, "It's Skunk,
he isn't moving, he may be *dying*! Please help, *quickly*!"

     The mice, who were generous and kind, raced
with him to the den.

        Coyote said, "You push, I'll pull,"
The mice were relieved that he was in front. They started
lifting the striped guy and moving him up the tunnel.
Suddenly Coyote bit Skunk's nose and Skunk released

his scent, which caused the mice to swoon.

Coyote pushed by and gobbled six. When he tried to get past Skunk again, Skunk said, "where are mine?" and turned his weapon.

Coyote coughed up three and said, "Just tenderizing them for you, heh, heh."

"This was a good idea," said Skunk between mouthfuls, "let's get a larger meal."

"Such as?" Coyote wondered.

"Deer, deer are dumb," Skunk said.

Coyote liked this guy.

"Okay, look," said Coyote, "we'll just reverse the game. I'll play dead here." and Coyote flopped down and Skunk ran off to the deer tribe in the field. "Help, Coyote has fallen and can't get up. I think he's dying."

A young fawn ran back with Skunk, the parents watching. When they got to Coyote, Skunk said, "We can push him back to his den, now push!"

And it was bite, spray, eat all over again. The partners were happy. But, Skunk had bigger plans, "Let's try Bear."

Coyote shrugged, Bear was not the sharpest pencil in the lunch box, but his meat was strong.

They planned, they executed, but Bear just sneezed and whupped their scrawny butts. Although Misses Bear found him hard to bear for a full moon.

Coyote at bat

"Look out, Coyote, rancher is on the warpath," Bat whispered, "seems he lost another cow when he came back after lunch."

"Yea, I know," Coyote smirked, "he was out to lunch for six months, one of the bovines tripped and landed on its head. I had a small meal from him since he was dead, and hunting wasn't that good. I may have left a footprint or tooth."

"He's going to leave a poisoned cow carcass for you."

"Thanks, I learned better than Wolf."

"But, Wolf didn't eat—"

"I Coyote triumphed due to excess and challenge.
Let Coyote eat the cattle and their cattle will become healthy.
Let him eat sheep and the sheep will benefit and thrive.
Rancher is stupid, unsuccessful. Coyote persists, prospers
and expands—"

"Which Coyote?"

"I was just speaking
in the third-person, me, Coyote continues to live in the dreams
of his admirers as the primordial teacher—"

"Who continues?"

"Never mind," Coyote sighed, "say, could you teach me
to hunt in the dark so no one could see me?"

"Sure," whispered Bat, "it's easy.
Here's the secret, as you run just make noise, a lot of noise,
and where the noise returns back to your ears, go
in that direction only. If you listen, you should be able
to hear the breathing of your prey. We'll try it tonight."

Later, that night, Coyote said, "Can you see the deer?"

"No, but I can hear it's echo."

"Whatever," Coyote sighed,
"can you point me and I'll start?"

Bat turned Coyote's head
and said, "Start running *now*! Bark **straight** ahead!"

And Coyote barked up a storm as he ran through the night.
Unfortunately, the deer was less dense than the saguaro
and Coyote brought down the cactus. He lay unmoving
and spoke to himself, "I am pierced. My head is split."

Coyote makes his mark

Coyote debates headsplitter

The setting: 'Coughing Eagle Memorial Puddle.'
The audience: Thirsty animals like Bobcat and Antelope.

    "You know," Dr. Vulture commented, "the archetypal
trickster is closely associated with the devil. Perhaps
they are the same, particularly in Christianity, where the devil
is the embodiment of pure evil, the scapegoat for our
self-loathing. Beginning as a playful trickster, he put on the mask
of a Serpent and reasoned with Eve to try
a golden delicious."

    Coyote ate a piece of corn tortilla.

    Vulture continued: "Why Joseph Campbell described Coyote
the trickster as a 'super-shaman' shaping the whole paleolithic
character. And Jung—"

    "Doctor Vulture? Turkey Vulture? May I call
you Turkey? No? What is a trickster but the hero of uncertainty,
the lover of ambiguity, and the creator of new ideas? Let us
honor me, umm the truckster, shower him, err me, with luxuries
and food. Let the paleolithic legend live in our *hearts* again!"

    "As I was saying," Dr. Vulture emphasized, "Jung
considered, regarding Psyche, that the unity of nature was in
the middle, and trickster was the figure of unity, creating
harmony, metaphorically a trickster discourse, between—"

    "Harmony?" Coyote interrupted, spraying tortilla chips.
"Here's your metaphor for harmony. I eat this corn, I chew
it and swallow it, then I sleep, then I shit, then I throw it
at your face, then I lick and smell it, and pronounce it good.
Your precious Gung also has argued that the trickster is
'undifferentiated energy' spinning through the universe, but I
focus my boundless energy on some poor sap, who has
to give me more food, so I don't have to run and chase it."

    "Look at *you* now! You are posturing for the audience, trying
to entertain, while I, Dr. Vulture, articulate the laws of lying.
Listen! There are three problems with lying, always. The first
is that your lies, which you meant to set you free

from the truth, can end up dominating you instead."

"So, what's
the problem, lies are lighter than truth and weigh less heavily
on the mind. Hey, dominate me."

"Well, another thing a life
of deceit demonstrates is that eventually your lies catch up
with you."

"No problem there, either. I have plenty of time. If
they catch up, I'll put them back in a bag," Coyote grinned.

Vulture was exasperated, "Finally, a trickster's deceitful
ways teach us that in the end we only deceive ourselves."

"Not a problem at all. Deceiving myself gives me pleasure
and lets me abide with stinking reality. And at least I respect
and love the deceiver. Deception keeps me healthy. I deceive
myself that the sun is warm and loving and will not burn me,
that the gentle breeze will not overturn me. If I gazed on naked
reality, unclothed with beautiful lies, I'd go mad."

"How sad. You cannot even recognize—"
"You ass, did you—"

"Don't commit the fallacy of *ad hominem*
with a personal attack—"

"You asshole, did you think that this
was a bloodless discussion with no consequences?"
Coyote snapped, pulling out some flight feathers and a small
piece of red flesh, "I can't improve my 'mythic fitness' by being
only positive. I had to invent death so there would not exist
only human beings and so that the continental islands
would not sink under their weight. That was clever of me:
I threw a stone into the stream; if it floated we would live
forever, if it sank, everyone would die eventually. I had to lie
to teach people the skills they needed to live: Caution,
like I did with deer, lies and loss, and that things are never
as they seem. I had to show them order and culture so that
they could cope."

"So, lying is good and necessary?" Vulture asked
as he jumped to a branch, glaring at a pulse in Coyote's throat.

"No, just entertaining. Hey, I see a mouse!"
and Coyote raced away.

Coyote deconstructs his myth

Taking his lead from the learned Doctor Vulture, Coyote decided to be educated. He put on a pair of glasses.

The Yellowjacket sisters seemed all abuzz, anticipating his new lecture at the 'Sneezing Lion Memorial Tree.'

Even owl was looking agog at Coyote's masterful presence. Turtle and Mountain Lion were there too, but they both seemed comatose or maybe just extremely contemplative.

"The trickster archetype," Senior Scholar Coyote started, while adjusting his glasses lower, "exists in many cultures. It is an old stereotype, older than the warrior, or king or wonder woman. Indigenes—new word, heh—have many stories of the trickster figure. This is so because we live in a dual reality of opposite polarities, such as good and evil, and Coyote only reflects that by exhibiting both tendencies. The Trickster capital 'T' is a valuable and necessary component of preter-human psychology. Without the trickster, your little lives would dull and perhaps unbearable. Yet, like everything else, the Trickster has a dark and a darker side, I mean light side," and Coyote held out his foreleg and rotated it so part was in shadow. "And that's the secret to that. Light, dark, it's just shadow of the same substance. Nothing to worry about folks. In this way we can give the trickster a more positive or lighter note," and Coyote raised his forelegs.

"Some Doctor Roangrim described the beloved Trickster as a false shaman, a source of satire on the excesses and abuses of shamanism. The heroic Coyote is clearly an object of satire and ridicule for this reason. He is portrayed as an incompetent charlatan who conjures phantoms that take energy from the tribe and his careless, evil manner reverses the traditional tribe-nurturing role of the shaman to serve his own needs. Evil? This is a sad distortion of the truth. When have I ever put my wants or momentary desires before your needs?" —One of the Yellowjacket sisters noted that Coyote's penis seemed to be more alert—

"Some Perfessor Shortgrizzle described Coyote as a bricoleur, a mythic handy-man who cobbles reality in the form

of a bricolage out of the available material, which is quite
everything when you think about. It is also the first stage
of a mythic creative process, providing the botched magic
with which trickster unwittingly constructs the bricolage that will
determine the realities of the world to come. Coyote's so-called
blundering attempts at secrecy not only fail, they set a mythic
precedent—Coyote exposes everything, especially to females—
and if what he achieves is not what he intended, it nevertheless
represents a *successful* shamanistic endeavor. The false shaman,
in fact, becomes the mythic shaman. Impotence is transformed
into *real power*, absurdity into true meaning, and the trivial
into the ceremonial consequential as Coyote the holy trickster
is unceremoniously—"

> "Which Coyote?" asked Bat, confused again.

"—shuffled from one role to another in a confusion of
ironies that is luminal, liminal, and subliminal, enlightening—"

Coyote paused, trying to decide if he was praising himself
enough. "Stories of tricky Coyote are not meant to be taken
seriously. They are always educational. Often the stories
are funny, very funny, sometimes scatological, rarely
offensively overtly sexual—after all, they are for children."
Coyote paused and looked wise, his glasses sliding a little.

"If a prostitute turns a trick, then Coyote is a Trickster.
Another trick, please. Quick," he said, smiling at Badger's
woman. "So, feed your inner Trickster, that is the lesson.
Do what you want. The symbolic trick has real ontological
significance when it acquires material existence," and
with that he defecated by the lectern.

Coyote changes Or One more trick sailor

Now, none of the women would have him, he thought,
but he knew that the men were, ah, less selective.
He had noticed some good-looking men, Bobcat and
Mountain Lion, for instance. There was even a new Coyote
on the edges of the territory. Coyote would do anything
for action. He sighed; maybe the professors were right.

Coyote took an elk's liver, warm and moist, and made
a vulva from it. Put it under his tail. Then he took two elk's
kidneys and made breasts from them. Put them on his chest.
Finally he put on a woman's dress. The Yellowjacket sisters
sewed him into the red dress, enclosed him very firmly.
He stood transformed into a very pretty woman indeed,
not on close inspection though. He put a fresh mouse
in the sleeve. He was ready. The girls buzzed their approval.

He walked down by the river, the liver chaffing his thighs.
but the dress swirled attractively. There beneath the pine
was the new coyote, as handsome as Coyote himself
and as full of himself. They talked, about the weather,
hot, and about the river, cool. Coyote waited for the other
handsome coyote to offer him—her now—a mouse.

He did. A plump mouse still alive, which Coyote gulped, then
remembered to say a sweet "Thank you." That male sure
was beautiful. Coyote was in love and ready to give
himself—if he could figure out how. He displayed his rear.
        The other Coyote seemed awkward, but it was over faster
than a human public road courting. They lay on the sand
under the shade, licking and snuffing and dozing.

Coyote was so pleased at the result that he flung
off his disguise and revealed his real masculine self.
            The other young male gazed admiringly, then shed
his own mask—Wakanda! His mate, mother of his *pups*!
This *sucked*! He had never been tricked, fooled, or so

humiliated, recently anyway. He threw his clothes in disgust
at the Yellowjacket sisters, who went in the sleeve
excitedly, and ate the mouse inside its fur.
          Coyote started to stalk angrily into the river, but
Wakanda grabbed his tail and pulled him back.
"You thought I was just a simple mother?"
she asked. "just good for a quick pump or cleaning up
the stuff from the pups? Huh?"
          Coyote snapped around but missed.
     She said, "I am just like you, a coyote, and I like to play
the games of life and death, just like you, just like the mother
of all pups."
          Coyote considered, "Why haven't I seen you before?"
     "You have," she said, "but I was always a male when you saw
me, of course a graceful, clever male, flawless—"
          "Okay, alright, I understand, but a female—
women cannot be tricksters. It is not *right!*"
     "Why? why not?" she demanded.
                         "*Mmfttthhh*,"
Coyote raged incoherently, "because females are good
or perfect. It is not goodness that instructs. Not perfection
that screws up everything to drive development."
          "Only a male would say that.
Females can hate and plot as ruthlessly as any coarse male.
You think that because you have your secret male
societies for hunting and gossiping that we do not?
We do. We can run or ruin a good thing as easily as you."
          Coyote shook his head and headed towards
the hills, but Wakanda nodded at the Yellowjacket
sisters, who stung him enthusiastically until he jumped
into the river.
          Wakanda came in and caringly soothed her mate,
"I can get some good mud for those, and we can talk.
I had a good day. How was yours? I was so attracted
by that cute red dress. Where did you get it?"
     And they talked by the river, two tricky beings
delighting only in themselves for the moment.

Coyote overextends himself **Or** Tricky dick in a fix

Coyote was watching Horse over on the mesa eating tender
shoots of bunch grass. Horse raised his head, locked
his legs and his penis extended almost to the ground
and released water in a stream.
                                    Coyote's eyes bulged.
'Have to get one of those' he thought, 'to impress
the hell out of those new young foxes by the water
hole.' He ambled on up to Horse and said "just noticed
the length of your member—
could I borrow it?"
                                    Horse snorted and said: "Ever
try to mount a mare? You need this pole just to get close
to the circle of—"
                         "I was thinking more for show,"
Coyote interrupted, "need to attract the attention
of someone."
                    Horse chewed and pondered, swallowed
the green morsels and noted: "Seen men, once, put
a plant shaft over their inches. See that boojum plant
in bloom? Above the white sage? Take the mast
and slide it over your shaft. That should get the girls
liquid! Now, go away, before I *kick* you!"
                    "Okay, okay." Coyote said, "I get the picture."
He slunk away, then out of sight pranced quickly
to the towering plant. He looked. He bit the spike,
then chewed and chewed it until it fell. Proudly
he surveyed his work. Getting it on, however,
was no mean feat. He had to lie on his side and use
his feet to slide the sharp hollow tube over his limp
hollow tube, the splinters making it limper.
Not exciting he thought, but he remembered the goal,
the plan, and the purpose of this suffering.

Finally, he slipped it off, getting splinters
the other way, then stood, put it on again,
then picked it up the middle in his teeth

and started towards the water hole. It was long
and awkward and knocked over a wasp's nest
and some flew in the end. They stung. He dropped it
on the ground for a rest. He got it up,
but his member had swelled from the stings
of the wasps. It was never coming off.

      When he got it to the water hole, he peeked
over the grease bush and saw two girls
standing talking, tails high, waiting for a male
to pass by. After weeks of grunting and groaning
Coyote got it up. He moved forward but it plowed
in the sand and stopped him, now too heavy to lift.

   Coyote remembered the time, however briefly
that his fur had been bright blue, like bluebird's
and he remembered stealing the sun. Now he was just
a father, a husband, a bread winner and den digger,
no longer the idol of young females everywhere.

      He would be again, if he could just move this
this pole thing. Simple physics. He levered it
up with another branch, but could not
move very fast. It looked like the girls were getting
ready to leave. He carefully picked it up in his teeth,
anchored by splinters on his penis. He trotted
towards the hole, then shouted, "Hey girls, look at
this!" but it fell from his mouth. Spirit, that hurt.
It bounced on the sand and pulled him down the slope
rolling, over and over. **Splash**!!

      The girls jumped in fear.
Conchita said, "What was that?" and Esmerelda answered,
"I don't know, but there isn't a female large enough—
the splinters alone—do you think he's alright?" she asked,
as they watched Coyote roll into the water, dragged down
by his pole. "Perhaps he thinks he's a swordfish. I don't
want to know."

     "Oh, he worships the instrument
and not the juice, the lingam and not—" Esmerelda giggled.
and they trotted back to the safe den of their parents.

From underwater, Coyote watched their tan and trembling
haunches recede from sight. He felt himself press against
splinters—it was hard to breathe and he could not move
or get it off. He sighed and watched the bubbles rise,
then started to chew a hole in the side for air. Slowly
the small end of the plant raised above the surface.
Water gutted out, then sharp breathing sounds.
 Gila woodpecker landed on the tip and started rapping
out his tune. Coyote groaned "get help" and started humming
in code, and woodpecker flew off straight to Gopher Tortoise,
whom he asked, "What can I do for this headache?"
  GT chewed meditatively and answered, "Stop using
your head and start heading your use. Give up beetles."

Coyote decided to pray. Shiva would know what to do,
being god of ecology and the young and the humble, like
Coyote himself. He might be away, though, in mysterious
India, directing traffic from an elephant or something wild.
 So Coyote thought he would pray to Hermes instead.
He knew he'd get action from Hermes, the god of one-night
stands, the patron of thieves, liars, and footloose
wanderers, and the guide for souls on their way
to the underworld, but Hermes didn't respond; perhaps
his nikes were wingless in those tight caves.
  Maybe Artemis, the keeper of the mysteries of death
as genesis of life, the lady of the beasts, would know,
could tell him what he should do. He could picture
her, now, babe of the beasts, skirt decorated with bees,
garlands of grapes above her breasts, strings of pale
bulls balls below them.
     He yearned for her, but she was
in the depths of her sanctuary, moaning about
the damage Coyote had done to the sacred
reputations of animals, gods, girls, myths,
and words.

Conquering Bombay Or Pass the masking tape

Recovering from his last hard adventure, Coyote had
good times watching sports on television, at least
until Renren opened his big almost fully-grown
mouth and told Coyote that the average pay
for a shot was eight thousand dollars, hit or miss,
play or not. After that, it was hard to root for anyone—
even the underdogs made seven.

That's all they saw anymore, millionaires
playing ball, or millionaires pretending to be Cleopatra
or Joe Louis, or millionaires playing or telling us
how much they could help their businesses.

Millionaires at work, millionaires at war, millineries
at parties, millionaires at home, with children—only
everyone tolerated them because they wanted to become
them, at least Coyote did, and so he hatched a plan.

Coyote knew he could become rich, but first
he needed a guide, someone who knew the ins
and outs, but first he had to piss like a Horse.
Coming back into the den, on TV he saw the actress slash
socialite slash tramp, Bombay Chevrolet, daughter
of the famous auto tycoon (who was famous for not
squandering all of his massive inheritance). Coyote knew
that he could have her, if he could get to the human city
of New York, which name sounded to his ears
like the asthmatic bark of a dying ground squirrel.
He would set out immediately, after rubbing
noses with the kids and Wakanda, and lying of course.

It took a while, even in this supersonic age, hitching
a ride on a sheep truck from Arizona to Virginia
then on a chicken truck from Harrisonburg
to Lewes Delaware. And from there, Coyote decided
to paddle a canoe to the island New York.

Coyote was paddling along the coast when
people called out from the shore: "Where you going?"
     "Going to have the daughter of Donald Chevrolet," he said.
      "Only a moron would do that!" they said.
    Coyote got mad, paddled in and turned them into chickens.
Then changed his mind and turned them into cows:
"You will be the cows that meatheads need to eat."
          He departed and went paddling. Pretty soon another
group of people asked: "Where you headed?"
     He told them. They said: "Be careful. The balls
of other men are piled in front of her lodge."
     Coyote appreciated this, so he came ashore and put
mussels and wild Atlantic salmon in the water by them,
then went on. At a place called Avalon, he put ashore
and walked through the pine trees to a large hotel. Saw
a wrinkled old woman steaming blue crabs. He grabbed some.
      "Coyote!" she smelled him, "what are you doing here?
why are you eating my crabs?"
                    Coyote looked at her
and said, "You know me?"
                    "Of course, you're famous. There
are books listing your legendary exploits with the peoples
of the continent."
                "There are?" Coyote asked. "Can you see
me? The real me? As I am, as an immoral trickster idol?"

She said 'yes, she was sensitive and clairvoyant.'
          Coyote shook his head, this would not do,
she must be in tremendous pain. He chewed
on some pine gum, then spit in her eyes.
    She became dumb and blind to the human comedy;
now, she was happy and thanked him. They talked about
where he was going. She warned him gently.
               He told her who he was going to marry.
     She said, "You be careful. She has a way
of making men go limp with mockery.
Take these pieces of rubber and when you are with
her, put them in your ears. Look deeply into her body

but not into her mind or heart, which are black holes
without light or warmth." To thank Coyote for his gift
of comforting dullness, she gave him also the masks
of a poodle, innocent girl, business consultant, and lawyer.
Coyote looked at them without understanding; they
were not like the masks of the wren, deer, goat, and bear
that he had used before. But, he could not refuse the gifts.
He put them in his kit, with the mask that Wakanda had made
for him, a human mask with silver hair at the temples, to give
him dignity; she had called it the George Hamilton mask.

Finally Coyote reached the territory of the Chevrolets,
the Trumps, Buffets, and Duponts. He put on the actor mask
to make himself look older. And sat by the river. Nothing
happened. He walked up the island, through the artificial
canyons and then circled a large park at the center.
Shortly—it must be fate—the daughter Bombay came by
with her friends Paris and Roma, and saw him.
      "He would make a good toy," she said, "let's take him back
to the condo and degrade him," which they did.
            That night she asked Coyote to come to bed with her.
Coyote could hear the sound of mockery from under her
tortured hair. Once in bed, he heard the sound of snickering,
so he put the rubbers in his ears and smiled at her,
reveling in her young frequently-advertised body. She mocked
him, but frowned when it had no effect. Safe sex at last.
He took off his mask and showed her that he was Coyote;
he had come to marry her. She agreed, thinking it was
a good career decision, and they tested the limits
of the bed, with screams and laughter.

When Donald Chevrolet heard laughter coming from
his daughter's room, he got up and came in. He said,
"Who is that with you, under the covers? Who's tail
is that?"
            She said: "That's my husband, welcome him."
      "Oh, please, spare me," said that Donald, and left.
The next morning Donald set a trap for Coyote, then knocked

on the door and requested Coyote to come out into
the cavernous breakfast nook to meet him.

Coyote put on the poodle mask and came out, to be caught
by one of the bodyguards, Steve, who tossed him over
the fortieth-story balcony.

Donald said, "Serves him right
for embarrassing me. Tell the doorman to clean up
the suicidal poodle's mess. And tell Bombie that 'fluffy'
couldn't stay." And he went out to an important business
meeting with his partners. Far below, on the busy street,
Coyote took off the flat poodle mask and took the elevator
back to the penthouse, back to bed with Bombay.

The next night Donald heard laughing, so he just sighed
and set another trap. When Coyote came out with
the innocent girl's mask, one of the body guards, Reggie,
grabbed him and arranged for him to sold to an exotic
service industry outlet, where he was reamed
until dusk by foreign businessmen—before he was flat
and totally dry, he took off the innocent's mask,
although he put it back on just long enough to get a cab
uptown. Bombay was having breakfast while her hair
was being trained. Coyote came in, feasted on strawberries
the real authentic food of the gods; they went back to bed.

For the third time, Donald heard sounds of love-making
and laughter and again knocked on the door and asked
who was with his daughter, now. Bombay answered,
"My husband, you know that."

Donald shrugged in disgust
and gave orders for another trap. When Coyote came out
the next morning in the consultant mask, the bodyguard
Ivan paused, as Coyote said, "Think about your career,
I have more power than Donald and I could have you fried."
Ivan held up his open paws and stepped back. Coyote sat
down to eat with a surprised Donald,

"I thought
you were some damned musician or Greek sailor,

perhaps I was wrong."

Coyote took the financial pages
and occupied himself. Donald sat plotting a new plot.
"What are you doing with those figures?" Coyote asked.
"Those are stocks. I am making them grow."
"How do you do that? Is it easy? Could I do it?"
"Maybe, here try. Punch in your numbers."

Finally, the Donald asked Coyote to come with him and work
on a new business venture over on Wall Street. They took
the limo to his office. They invested in a venture that
Donald was sure would break Coyote. Coyote picked
up a stock certificate and chewed it quietly. Donald
asked Coyote to meet his obligations. When
the call came, Coyote was trapped by declining values.
He spat out certificates, and Donald thought Coyote
was through, hemorrhaging red ink. He said, "Serves
you right for trying to marry my daughter without
my permission," and was escorted to the limo.

Coyote left the ruined consultant mask on the trading floor,
put on the lawyer's mask and raced out to the limo,
"Why did you leave me, dad, I was almost trapped?"
"Oh, my fortunate son, so glad to see you, almost cried
myself to death when I realized that you had been ruined.
I thought, how was I going to tell my daughter? How did
you get out by the way? That's not possible."
They got into the limo and started home. Coyote was
chewing on a piece of shoe leather. When it was soft he carved
a policeman and threw it out the window, saying, "You
shall be the law." The law followed and grabbed Donald
as he got out of the limo.

"Get my *lawyer!*" Donald shouted.
Coyote gave his card to the law and said, "I'm his lawyer.
I'll see my client tomorrow." When Coyote got back
to the penthouse, Bombay asked where he father was.
Coyote said he didn't know for sure, probably at the club.

Coyote makes his mark on Wall Street

Coyote signed the papers for the psychiatric assessment
of Donald and quietly assumed responsibility for running
the Chevrolet corporation. His first decision was to push
a car called the 'Coyote' to compete with the Cougar,
Mustang, and Viper (when Wakanda heard, furious that it was not
named after her, she stole a Miata for herself).

With sixteen cylinders, it was so overpowered, 1200 HP, in
the first three gears that it caused numerous accidents and had
to be retired to the pantheon of Edsels and Thunderbirds.
Regardless of his inability to create a popular, efficient car,
Coyote ran the nonprofit foundation quite well, getting many
more animals, including coyotes, protected by the EPA.

Furthermore, he was able, working with Dirt First and other
human groups, to get Eastern Arizona made into a corporation
with a board of directors that included several snakes
(the original kind, thus decisive and responsible) so
the desert would be protected forever. He even
started a youth club called the Coyscouts of Arizona,
who were really good at survival training.

Bombay tired of him, but could not dislodge him
from the penthouse or corporate offices. She screamed
that he was nothing but a cheap coyster bent on stealing
her family's fortune.

He was bent though. Coyote had a short
affair with Roma but had forgotten to put rubbers in his ears—
she wanted her little coytoy, her ruffy-wuffy coybow,
to appreciate her voice and her lust for him—

he had forgotten how consuming the human tongue—
but by then he had a new mistress, power. Power.

He understood in his sly way that corporations had to please
their stockholders. His bodyguard Ivan counseled him
on entertainment and understanding of the lowest common
denominators of life, as if Coyote had never been so low.

Coyote knew what to do. He knew everything better

than anyone, so he never asked for no advice nohow.
He invested in a series of semi-domestic coyotes he called
'coyopets.' but they bit children and had to be recalled.
    The series of transformer machines, called 'coybots,'
did marginally better, before they were recalled.
    "I have to get richer," Coyote was saying to Crow,
his most recent guest in the Boardroom, "maybe something
really cheap and simple—"
        Crow asked Coyote, "Why do you
want to be richer?"
            "For food, silly, and women, and finer furs, in
richer colors. Why do you birdbrains hide from wealth?"
    "I don't need to hide. Wealth avoids me. Poets can never
get rich selling their works, because everyone sees
themselves as poets, not being able to create pet rocks
or other technological accomplishments. No. A verse
is a gift; it cannot be otherwise, as it has no value, but it has
obligation, the obligation to reciprocate or to change."
    'Hmm,' Coyote thought, and had Crow shown out the door.

The prices of houses sky-rocketed so people could not afford
them, and then the bubble collapsed. Countries called in debts
to forestall their fiscal slide. Conditions seemed bleak.
Coyote analyzed the downturns of the market and identified
some trends—after the civil war the public turned to circuses
for succor; after the depression, people lost themselves
in movies; after the bush league years, video games sucked
in the souls.
        Knowing that 2006 was going to hit bottom,
Coyote had the corporation sell off its cars to Kia
and invested exclusively in interactive holographic movies.
"Coyovision" took off—he was richer than Croesus or Gates.
Although horror themes proved irresistible, the remake
of a roadrunner cartoon—a different roadrunner
eaten each time, unable to escape from Coyote's clever
cars or rockets, unable to avoid capture—proved
to be uninteresting to kids or to mature consumers,
so Coyote remained unknown and unworshiped

behind the new corporate logo 'Chevroplay.'
Then things changed in unexpected ways;
people no longer wanted to work to buy more things
at least beyond the 'Coyovision' wall unit.
Instead of rebuilding, instead of starting the up cycle
the economy stayed at the curved, stable bottom.
Without being creative people tired of their toy.
Coyote had undermined the last dignities of civilization.
It was time to enron out. Leaving the deserted city,
he paused to piss on the corner of the building
at the corner of Wall Street.

Coyote trips, civilization falls

This was no fun, no fun at all. He went back to Arizona
because things were going to be really difficult now
and he needed to have a safe and secure place
to dwell in the colorful and comfortable desert.
From time to time, he ran into Fox and Bluejay,
who seemed to be traveling to a clean place also.

At a deserted gas station on 18, where the last sign
said nine dollars a gallon, he rolled in oil to get
the colors from light to reflect in his fur
for his triumphant homecoming to Wakanda
but Wakanda gagged and made him bathe.
 She said the pups had grown and moved to Seattle
and she Wakanda was ready for more.
 Coyote knew he was in trouble
when he saw she was wearing the mask
of the handsome male, the mirror
coyote that Coyote loved.

Meanwhile people became less interested in working
and making things they did not need, more interested
in talking to other people, and enjoying life,
and so things fell apart. 'So what,'
thought Coyote, just another cycle down.
 Many people left the cities; some stayed and started
growing food on rooftops. People flooded to farms
and overused the land and left, but a few stayed
and started permacultures. Some fled
to the forests and deserts, but could not make
the land provide, after killing off antelope
and even eating rattlesnakes fried in oil.

Devastated, Rattlesnake crawled to ask Vulture, "What—"
 And that was all the good Doctor needed:
"—is the moral of all this, that Coyote has done?
You ask, you were asking that of course.

There is no moral, none, nothing, no meaning, no tragedy.
Things just happen that might have happened anyway.
Good causes evil, evil causes good, then all that
fervor decays into the fertile soil for more life, which goes
on, sometimes questioning itself
sometimes not—"
               "But Coyote, he made things worse."
    "Oh, for you maybe, but not in the long run;
he just mixed things up, added to the soil. Well,
he shit on everything and shit is good, it fertilizes
soil—"
       And Rattlesnake coiled and started rattling,
so Doctor Vulture lifted lopsidedly above the Palo Verde
above its exquisite blue blossoms and said:
     "I know, your sorrow is not lessened or diminished;
it is real and painful, and you can follow the chain
of events from Coyote to the death of your young.
    Why not just bite Coyote and feel better—
who knows, things might get better now."
and Vulture circled up, spiraled way above
the desert floor on a column of rising air.

Unknown to them, in the next valley away, Coyote lay
flat, dusty and unmoving—

                   (The end? Oh, sure, you *wish*!)

Coyote goes to war Or *Privates on parade*

Just as the sun was teasing the desert, a cactus flower
exploded!

        Exploded? Coyote wondered, then the *boom*
buffeted his ears. Coyote felt a hot wind, then dove
for the sand. After a moment, he looked around. No
one. He crawled over the sand. No one, but he could
smell something. His ears went to full alert. Noises
two hills away.

On the next slope, he found another coyote, dead.
He crept stealthily to another hill, peaked over:
Three human beans, with some strange machine.
Coyote did not understand the purpose of that thing;
the victims were not eaten; why kill them but not eat
them? Something was wrong here.

Coyote watched a soldier dance the status dance;
the group automatically divided according to power.
They were like wolves, Coyote thought, sniffing
each other's butts to see who had higher rank.
Maybe he could find another den warmer among
those metal riches. He could hear them talking.

"Project COYOTE is a success, it seems."

                            "Coyote, sir?"
"I never explain myself, Captain, but just in case
someone is reading this abominable claptrap, it's
Counter Operational Yoke for Obstructionist
and Terrorist Entrapment"

                  "But, why real coyotes, sir?"
    "Dammit, man! Stop asking nonsense!" Colonel Cornpen
barked, "I hate enlisted people. Sneaky, stupid,
devious little bastards just like that animal, coyote,
only I can't use you for target practice, so I have
to use coyotes—perfect practice organisms. Besides
there are way too many of them according to the local

ranchers, who are donating extra money to me to remove
them from the cattle range. It's a win-win situation
obviously, for the military. Turn the WAM BAM ADD-ONS
twenty degrees west there and *fire* it up!"

"Wham, sir?"

"Wake up, warfighter, you should know this stuff:
the Weapons for Arbitrary Mass-destruction
and the Biological Amplification Monitor for the
Acoustic Detection, Destruction Or Neutralization System.
I rarely explain myself, warfighter, but just in case
someone else isn't saluting this parade of letters, we
are focusing sound waves that turn coyotes into puddles
of drool. Now, turn up the sound. Sergeant, go
to deaf-con one, ha! Now hit it! The red button, boy,
the red for dead button! *Hit it!!*"

Coyote stood up to see more just as the beam
of sound mixed his nuts and flattened him.
A few insects and birds fell out of the sky behind
the ruined, lifeless carpet of mangy fur.

"Another hit! What was the range?"

"Three hundred
meters, sir. Is this part of project UP-URS, sir?"
    "What?"
        "UP-URS, sir!"

"*Damn!* Oh, yea, Urban Pacification—
Using Reducing Sound. Yea, WAM BAM UP-URS, coyote,
heh, heh, heh. Don't risk that again, boy. Go thirty south."

in a CUNT (Complex Underground Networked Terrain)
nearby, Coyote was shuffling through a pile of
masks, until he found the one he needed, the DICK
(Duplicitous Innovative Cereal Killer) mask.

Moving gracelessly, but with human dignity, closer,
Coyote noticed the neat pelts and shiny baubles
of the soldiers, as well as the array of clever things

that some of them commanded others to work.
He noticed the rank of some of them. He wanted to be
the alpha male of that pack. Coyote put on the George
C Scott mask and went to work.

"Son, you there," commanded the ramrod straight officer,
"help me off this rock!"

                    "Sir, General, *sir!*"

"Latrans, General Latrans. Get Cornpen for me!"

                                        "Colonel

Cornpen, sir?"

            "The same. *Now!* And get me a bottle of water."

    "*Sir!* Yes, sir, **sir.**"

Down in the dry wash, Fox was helping an oddly deflated
Coyote try to round up animals to make a military fighting
Force, but it wasn't working—

                        "We can't fight those

monsters," Badger said.

                    "What? Don't whisper! Badger,
please, stop digging and listen, coyotes are being killed,
killed over the next ridge!"

                    "So, what can we do?
No badgers are being killed are they?"

            Then, Coyote lay down and snuffled in the dirt,
looking at the vultures circling above in the sky.

    Elfowl came up and volunteered, saluting smartly,
"I'll go with you."

                "Alright, you start out. I have to get
my secret weapon in the den."

                "And elfowl flew straight up and straight out.

"General?"

        "Latrans, Colonel, we met at MisCom games."

    "What are you doing here?"

                    "Inspecting you," Coyote
barked. "I'm from COOT."

            "Coot, sir?"

"Surprise, Colonel,
I don't always explain myself, but in case anybody is reading
this rubbish, the Commission On Unconventional Threats—"
"Shouldn't that be spelled with one 'o' sir?"
"Do you love your country, better than spelling, colonel?
Of course you do. Aren't we both here to defend freedom?
Of course we are. I'm here to assess project SNUF—"
"snuf?"
"SNUF, sir, to you, Systems for Neutralizing Undefined
Foes, an arm of DUST—don't ask, Destruction of
Uncooperative Surface Targets. Now, tell me what you have
here. Show me how it works."
"Sorry, sir, it's classified."
Colonel Cornpen hedged.
"Not from me it's not! Not from SNUF!"
"Sir, yes sir, we detect sonic vibrations, identify azimuth, range
and elevation, then focus horrifically amplified sound waves
on that point—"
"And why aren't we testing them on people?
the homeless, illegal aliens or the Irish?"
"You know why, sir, we got caught
and besides, life is sacred, that's why we started POW—
Protection Of Warfighters," he translated automatically,
"Yes, Colonel, I remember, POW from BOOM," Coyote
said, automatically expanding the phrase, Bio-Organisms Of
Murder, "but what about ants?"
"ANTS, general? You mean
Artificial Natural Terminating Systems? I know what—"
"Ants, idiot. They're biting my *foot*! Look, Colonel, the sound
system is still on; can I use it to project my voice?"
Just then Elfowl got tired and landed
on the red button. Coyote reached for the boom, but tripped
and the machine swung in a complete circle, within
the three hundred meter range, on the soldiers, who danced
the perfect death dance and all fell over immediately,
with expressions like they had just heard Chingy for a third
time, and lay quiet, small red threads dripping from their
loosened orifices.

91

Elfowl saluted. Coyote continued talking, although
only he and owl could hear: "No, dipshit, I meant ants, army
ants, desert army ants, and they should all be here in a few
minutes to eat up all this extra protein. I guess I'll just retire,
now. Good-bye." he and owl saluted again and he carried
the shiny machine back to his den.

Coyote was lying in his den discouraged by this new threat,
when a high-ranking army officer came striding in, dragging a
strange piece of equipment. "You!" Coyote barked. But,
the other took off his mask and a beautiful male Coyote stood
revealed. "*You!*" Coyote shouted. And the other Coyote took off
his mask and Wakanda stood there smiling. "**You**! Not again!"
Coyote snuffed.

       "What could I do?" Wakanda asked. "You were
lying flat as a tortilla and I was worried. Are you alright?"
       Coyote hung his head, "No one would join me.
I would have fought them, coulda beat them," he snuffled.
     But Wakanda was looking at her masks, "I always wondered
what would happen if you put a mask over a mask. You only
did one at a time, but I was in a hurry to infiltrate the enemy
and deconstruct it with a little chaos—well, no, because
it was fun to make trouble and to play with their toys."
                        "Well,"
Coyote admitted, "it did some good for the community.
Could we use that thing to get a mouse?"
    Wakanda scratched a circuit chip and the thing went dark.
then she noticed someone standing in the corner,
"Who's that?" she asked.
          "It says exoskeleton,"
Coyote said, "found it on a deaf soldier by the den.
He said it was for performance augmentation to extend
a mission payload, using proteinaceous organic fluids.
I think we could use it for—"
          Wakanda squealed and ran,
understanding its applications for power mating.
     Coyote decided to try three masks at once next time.

Coyote gets religion Or *Pass the salve*

"Jesus, hear my words, heal my wounds, come to me
and show me the way from this barren
desert—"
            'Barren desert?' Coyote wondered, crunching
the bones of a mouse, and looking at the straggling man
on the top of the hill. 'This is paradise, with food
and warmth for everyone.'
      Who was this man ordering a great spirit
to wait on his infirmity and weakness?
Coyote listened: 'The devil made me do it!' alibi
tripping off the tongue with oiled practice. Coyote decided
to make an appearance.

Coyote was able to find his graham cracker
mask at the bottom of the pile in old den number 26.
      He went back to talk to this man
who was getting sunburned by the saguaro.
      "Jesus?" the man asked.
                        "No." answered Coyote,
"Just a simple seeker of truth, like you."
                  "Wow, you were coming from the direction
of the sun and it looked like you had a halo.
Funny thing it was. Are you a Christian man?"
                        "I am from an older tradition," Coyote
answered, "where the exact flavor of the jam
does not matter, as long as the toast
is buttered."
            "I'm sorry, I don't understand.
Let me learn from you, master. When
can you teach me, when can you help me?
My name—"
                  "—doesn't matter. I don't care."
      "Truly you are wise and are showing me the way
to break the cycle of ownership of things and words."
                  Coyote almost spoke, but decided to listen.
Coyote gave the man some lotion.

Coyote thought, he could give him religion, too,
the religion of Coyism, the way of lettings things flow
as things flow to and through the coyote gut.
          Coyote not only goes with the flow
but he pisses in it to make it run higher;
he could touch the bean of beans.

After a few days of silence, the man smiled
and left, leaving a few dry turds,
pieces of old skin and his white shirt.

Coyote soon worried that the animals were not religious
enough, except for Mountain Lion and Mantis.
Time for him to offer a prayer:
'Pray for prey, pay for prey, pray for pay,
give it to me, now. Now!' Too simple he decided.

Coyote wrote down some sayings to give to the animals
so that they could rehearse them:
          'Wisdom cannot be saved or explained.
    War never solves anything for long
          but peace makes for very poor reading.
And so, let Coyote lead the way in warning
that any imperative, from holy sex to violence,
cannot be allowed to run away
so that it overwhelms common sense and fair play.
    The best soldier is not brave. The best teacher is not smart.
    The most charitable person is not giving.
    The best writer does not use words,
          the best animal cannot help leaving turds.
      The fullest puddle is not full. The spent penis is not empty
and it cannot be exhausted. The deepest humility
is not much compared to dirt, water and mud.
      The greatest accomplishment always needs to be redone,
often on a weekly basis.'

Coyote reflected, then emptied his mind,
and slowly danced the dance without motion.

When knowledge and cleverness arrived
great deceptions were practiced
and when great deceptions were practiced
Coyote was there to lead the way,
for in deceiving yourself you make
yourself happy. In cheating yourself
you avoid the depressing world of truth.
No wonder humans are depressed. They know.
   These were the words Coyote spoke
and these are the words the animals
misinterpreted to mean that they could lie
and always be happy.
        'Those who try to grasp
Coyote cannot hold him for he flows like water.
The highest good is making water
           which he calls coyotea.
Coyote is not straight for he is like his water
making runnels in the sand becoming a hundred rivers
and filling the entire oceans, overcoming logs
and mountains, before returning to the skies.
Touch the Coyote penis and the most gentle thing becomes
the most hard, but graceful fluids can overcome the hard
if they are true. Coyote celebrates the female
but knows the male and uses it to his advantage,
but for the good of all,' he said to an attentive cactus.

Coyote went looking for a willing convert.
   Soon, Badger was digging for mice and throwing
them to Coyote, who let them go. Badger asked
him, "What *good* is this new religion?
how does it help us live in this sandy paradise?"
    Coyote pointed to an old ruined wheel and said:
"The hole in the middle of thirty spokes
cannot go anywhere without the wheel. Be the hole.
Cut windows in a room and Coyote can take
your things. If everyone is good, then Coyote cannot be evil.
If there was no laughter, there would be no Coyote."
    "What was that about a hole?" Badger asked.

"And, what about snickering?"

Coyote spoke: "The emptiness of a wastebasket
makes it useful to hold the useless waste
of all the tired poorly-written Coyote myths."

Badger ate a mouse, contemplating its taste.

Coyote watched, and pronounced: "The coyote that
can be a taxonomic specimen is not the true
absolute absent eternal Coyote.

Coyote does not teach, but people are reformed
Coyote does not invest, but people become rich
Coyote has no ambition, yet people become peaceful
Coyote does not move, yet everything changes."

"What people? Us? Me? Am I rich?" Badger asked.

"I'm hungry," Coyote noticed, "is that all the mice?"

"What shall we call it? Church of the Skulking Scavenger?"
Badger asked.

Why did he let the mice go? Coyote thought,
and started digging.

Coyote on the moon Or **Out to launch**

One night, after he had stopped singing
under the clouds, Coyote watched the light.
Coyote saw hummingbird fly to the moon,
flying straight up beyond the ironwood tree
through the ringed clouds
and disappearing in the distance. Coyote waited
and wondered. When hummingbird returned
Coyote asked him what it was like.
　　　　　Hummingbird said, "Just like the desert, except
it is easier to fly—in fact, you could fly just
like me, if you could get there."
　　　　　　　　　　　　　　'There,' thought
Coyote, 'if I could get there.' He thought a few men
had gotten there on new things, new wings
and he Coyote had a unquenchable thirst for newness.
　　　　Coyote starthrower had flung the stars there
long ago, but they had changed and rearranged.
An idea formed and the pine-sap yellow eyes narrowed
and focused on the horizon . . .
　　　　　　　Wings—but first lose weight and get in shape.

Interludes

The deer diet Or *Bite me*

"Deer and his wife Dear have invited us to dinner tonight.
Are you going to clean up," Wakanda asked her mate.

"Ritual purification is necessary before any meal with Deer,"
Coyote answered. "Besides, I think Deer wants to thank
me for showing him the Middle Way."

"I don't remember that,"
she said.

"Well, remember that once Deer was so strong
and fast, leaping from mountain top to mountain top, that no
one could catch him, until a Palouse woman, probably one
that I made, threw a breech clout on his hind end to slow
him down. Problem was then he became too quiet and peaceful,
chewing his cud, so that anyone, even a woman, could club
and eat him."

"And, what did you do to alarm him?" she asked.

"I just backed my rear end into his nose. He snorted and ran,
and ever since only those who prepare with a good sweat bath
can get close enough to kill him. It was a good deed, I think,
the act of a true friend." Wakanda snorted despite herself.

At Deer's home in the hillside grove, the Coyote couple
were welcomed by the Deer couple. They all sat apart from
the grass beds, enjoying the evening breeze. Coyote had to piss
right away and Deer nodded downhill. When he got back Deer
was already feeding Wakanda some of his own flesh and blood.

Coyote sat and waited patiently, discussing the politics
of the forest with the wife, Dear. After Coyote ate, they sat
and looked at the stars, which were bright and many. They talked
about the latest escapades of Turtle and Raven. Coyote invited
the couple to dine at their den the following week.
They went home before the eye-star set.

"Welcome to our home," Wakanda offered the Deer family—
they had brought two fawns with them.

98

"It's really comfortable, and so cool underground," said Dear, "Thank you for inviting us."

They went in to a low table set with green leaves, each sitting in front of a leaf. The almost-grown pups, Denny and Renren were already sitting.

"Should be a real banquet," said Deer.

"Just a minute, I invited Dr. Vulture and Eagle—" Coyote said, "famous noble Eagle himself, symbol of carrion-eaters and nations, now—to dinner, also, and they are arriving, I hear the whisper of feathers, ah!"

Vulture and Eagle wobbled in and sat in front of leaves, Eagle at one seat of honor, by himself.

Both fawns ate their leaves.

"As host, I am going to serve you from the wife," Coyote said, and headed towards Wakanda with a sharp blade.

Wakanda ran immediately.

Coyote started to give chase but then saw Denny, saying, "Or perhaps some flesh from the child."

Denny and Renren caught and passed Wakanda outside. The birds watched with interest, but Deer spoke, "Please, there is no need for us to take any of your family. We are vegans after all, and the leaves are great."

Dr. Vulture clacked and said, "I am hungry," looking at Deer with unmoving eyes.

Coyote brought out several old mouserolls but they were not enough for Vulture and Eagle. So, Coyote sighed and cut some meat from his own legs, which is why coyote legs became so skinny.

When Vulture and Eagle were full, they thanked Coyote and flew off to look for a desert dessert.

Dear took her kids and left, not talking to Coyote.

Coyote sat down next to Deer, who hooved Coyote's rear end further away. "It was a nice gesture, but you should have asked your wife first. Why don't you both come over next week and we can provide food for you again?"

"Spoken like a true friend, Deer. Look, I saved some fermented berries for us.

Got them from Woodpecker last week. Here, chew
on these!" Pretty soon, they were both rolling and laughing,
having forgotten the awkwardness of dinner.

"I have a hunch,"
Coyote said.

"Haunch, yes" Deer replied, and they both laughed.

"Seriously, I think we can get rich on this one." Coyote
narrowed his eyes.

"Oh, no, have you forgotten the armless
tee-shirt farce?" Deer asked.

"Oh, yea, only Rattlesnake bought
one. I used the rest to clean up the pups when I ran out
of saliva."

And they both kept laughing.

Finally, out of breath, Coyote said,
"Really, this is a food product. It is raw meat wrapped in rice and
seaweed and served cold as small medallions.
It will be elegant. I'll call it meashi. All we need is
a boundless source of raw meat—"

But, by then Deer had departed.

The plot against Trickster

Stinkbeetle started the meeting: "I cannot stand it any longer, the constant stepping on, nosing, flipping over, pawing— it's just too *much*!" After he calmed down and released some other vapors, he continued: "I know many of you have had problems with Coyote. I suggest that we form an association of like-minded animals to deal with the Coyote problem."

Cactusmouse nodded and squeaked: "Too true, why look at Lichen over there, so chewed that he cannot talk, treated like bubblegum by Coyote, then spit out."

"Wait," said Groundsquirrel, "it isn't coyotes that are the problem, just the immortal immoral big 'C' and I don't know how we can control him."

Elfowl turned his head and watched Groundsquirrel. "I too have been victimized by that humpback hitdog," added vice mayor Peccary, "If we just do something, what can it hurt?"

"What do you suggest?" asked Stinkbeetle.

"I would say start a campaign to discredit coyotes, picture them as unsanitary, violent dogs that need to be controlled, trapped and euthanized, to protect the smelly walky-talkers. Dogcatchers have everything in place and the experience." Peccary concluded.

"Perhaps an anti-Coyote association?" volunteered Elfowl, his head following whoever was speaking.

Peccary answered, "Less negative, I think. How 'bout Coyote Victims Anonymous. I also would prefer not to be known as a victim of Coyote or against him. Hmmmm."

"Hmm," echoed Cactusmouse, "Could we go high-tech with our strategy?"

"What do you mean?" asked Peccary.

"I mean sterilizing female coyotes to keep numbers down."

Groundsquirrel replied, "maybe a female robot to keep Coyote occupied might work. That's high-tech enough."

"We could ask Coralsnake about a restraining order; he knows the rules of the desert."

suggested a wary Peccary, noting that they were all exposed out in the daylight, "Mayor Turtle should be involved."

Stinkbeetle suggested that they schedule another meeting.

Elfowl wanted to name the association and a committee right away.

Peccary said to wait for Turtle and Coralsnake.

Stinkbeetle suggested that they do both, then if there were legal problems, they could be fixed later.

Elfowl said, "I like the whole CVA thing, let's go with that, and Stinkbeetle could be the chair."

"I see no problem with that," agreed the flattered Stinkbeetle, "Are there nominations for the committee?"

"I think we should wait for the others," said Peccary, "but I would not be against doing something concrete now."

Elfowl said, "I nominate Stinkbeetle, Groundsquirrel, and Peccary as the interim committee of leaders. Shall we vote? All in favor?" There were positive noises. "Opposed?"

Peccary only said, "I'll abstain rather than oppose. Would the committee please address the possible physical and legal actions?"

And, so the plot to control Coyote began to mushroom.

Really dead Or One jump away from fertilizer

Coyote was tired of being poor, tired of having to jump
on mice for a living. His mistress had said he was too cheap
to buy her what she needed and those criticisms hurt
the sensitive carnivore. He had to accumulate symbols
to trade to others for their work. And, he knew how.

      He would sell something that was not his, to get money
to make something else his. And, his new thing was
to be a forest In northern Idaho.

How would he buy and sell?
                    "Mineral rights," said Coralsnake.
"That way you can buy the land and do what you want
right away. I'll need ten percent for my help, of course."
           "Of course," said Coyote.

Coyote surveyed his forest outside of Potlatch, bought
from a family getting divorced, so sad of course.
As he admired the trees, they became slashes growing
through real dollar signs. He signaled to the local loggers,
who started their saws and started dropping every tree.

A bearded fellow with a black tee-shirt accosted him,
"You're raping the earth goddess,"
                      "No, just mussing her hair
playfully," joked Coyote. "Get lost before you get hurt,"
and Coyote started his own 72-inch bar saw.
Soon the trees were converted to cash.

Fondling his money, Coyote waited for the trees to spring
back, but they didn't. It had been three years, now.
The soil was still dusty. and runnelled.
                  "They won't comeback, you know,
for a long time," said a voice from behind.
      Coyote turned and saw the bearded shirt, Dirt First.
    "Because your wealth had to be immediate, you killed
all the trees, drove away the animals, let the fungus dry up.

The forests cannot be reborn without fungus and animals,
and the soil and water that is made by a forest."
        Coyote said, "Nonsense. Anything can be reborn."
  "Not in our lifetime. It's gone," and t-shirt walked away.
Coyote laughed and crumbled some dirt into dust, frowning.

Four years later, the land was still bare and dusty.
     Coyote was not happy.
The money was gone and there was nothing to sell.
He only wanted to profit from a little death and still
have it be alive. He spoke to the lifeless soil of the former forest,
"Why can't you be the way you were? Fertile, tree-bearing?"
     But, the dust was silent.

Tired of his umproductive unprofitable land, Coyote decided to go
downriver and amuse himself with one of the Nez Perce women.
As he approached he saw them. "Wait for me," called Coyote.
"I'll go swimming with you." He took off his jacket beaded
with shells that identified him as a great chief.
                    "We don't want to wait,
we are having a good time without you," replied the two women
as they danced on into the river.
            When Coyote joined them, they
pushed him down into the water and drowned him.

Later, Coyote's partner, Fox, appeared from around a bend
in the river, looking for something to eat. When he looked
into the river and saw something lying on the bottom, he said,
"Could *that* be Coyote?!" Fox pulled out the inert lump,
and when he was sure it was Coyote, he made a magical jump
over him and brought Coyote back to life.
     Coyote said, "Oh, I must have had a long sleep."
  "Not sleep, you were *dead*," replied Fox. "Why did you go near
those women? You had no right, they are from the Shell tribe."
     "How can you do that? Bring me back to life I mean?"
  "Spirit told you to vanquish the man-eating monsters who
were destroying the people that Spirit wanted to increase;
that was to be your work. He gave you the power to kill

the monsters, and he gave me the power to restore you to life
should you be killed. Your bones may be scattered; but if
there is one hair left on your body, I can bring you back to life.
By the way, Spirit despised you. He thought you would never
do any good. Your flesh is inedible and your name is degraded."

    "Thanks, I needed to know that. But, I got some
of the monsters." Coyote climbed part way up the hill and set
the grass on fire. The women did not escape and even their shells
were burned, which is why some shells have a black side today.

A few weeks later, a hunter, Sam McHooter, restaurant impresario
and entrepreneur, was looking for a bear or deer to shoot,
but someone had overlogged the whole forest and there
was nothing to kill. Then, he saw a tawny shape in the dirt,
a sleeping cougar he thought, and blasted away at it.
The pelt was too mangy, even where it was not ripped
with holes. So, he left it and hiked back to the jeep.

Fox came by, many moons later and found the holey pelt.
Recognizing the fur patterns, he jumped over it and brought
it to life. Coyote opened his eyes, and saw Fox, and said,
"Dead again? How long this time?"
                                   Fox rubbed his teeth against
his inside lips and said, "Dunno, maybe two to six moons."
                   Coyote licked where holes had been; it still itched.
"I think someone wants me dead. Could you check on me
every week? I could lose a lot of time every time they are
successful."
             Fox said, "Sure, you bet, but I'll need some food,"
looking at Coyote's legs, wondering if the stories were true.
                      "Yes, sure, food." Coyote sighed.

At the next CVA meeting, under the old cottonwood tree,
there was a spirited discussion about the recent temporary
deaths of Coyote. They decided to remove Fox from the picture.
In fact, they wanted him elsewhere, so they arranged with Eagle
to get him a job in California, something about television,
movies and media. It was the Twentieth Century after all.

FBI agents Or Don't need no stinking badgers

Coyote knew he would have to find out who was after him and put a stop to it. But, his nose could only reach so far. He needed professional help, and he knew where to get it.

Underground, in the Feral Burrow of Investigation, at Dead Rock, minds were being made up. "We have to look into Coyote's deaths. And, Coyote is alive again for the moment and wants to be part of the organization. What should we do?" Bobcat asked.

"He is the Elvis of animals, not some vague ass entertainer; he can get us notoriety, and legitimacy. Come on, it's only a badge and a piece of paper." Said Zebralizard.

"But, it's Coyote, he will eat the paper, comb his tail with the badge and try to mate with the awards committee!" exclaimed Grasshoppermouse.

Zebralizard capitulated, "Okay, we'll make it honorary, with no powers and no equipment. Maybe his involvement will flush the perpetrators from hiding?"

Bobcat said okay and Grasshoppermouse shrugged his consent.

"Are you ready to be sworn in, future agent Coyote?"

"Future honorary agent," Grasshoppermouse corrected.

"Yes," Bobcat and Coyote said at the same time.

"Then I want you to take the oath of fealty and perform the loyalty dance with me," said Bobcat.

All the members danced, holding their ties as they did. Coyote wondered how this group could even find their tails; still, their reputation was good and Coyote was offal, er, official, now. He was ready to investigate.

Coyote left Dead Rock and went far into the mountains. Soon he saw a mountain sheep. The sheep insulted Coyote, calling him stick-legs, which made Coyote angry. Coyote grabbed him and threw him against a ponderosa

pine tree so hard that the body went clear through
the tree, up to the head, which stuck out, with its horns,
like a bizarre trophy.

                    Coyote went "Humpf,"
and hung his Burrow coat on it. He sat down at the foot
of the tree and started to think: Maidens, hunters, what
did they have in common? Humans? How could his death,
the death of a legend, benefit any of them?

     Maybe if he went meditating—observing or fishing—
he would think better.

Wolf & man observed

Coyote was watching Wolf argue with Man. Coyote noticed that Man stood like a bear, while Wolf seemed to cower. Coyote knew men walked upright like Bear and that wolves lost most encounters with bears over food. Wolves expected to lose to bears and thus they expected to lose to men. Coyote was about to suggest to wolf that he stand to make the debate more equal.

He heard Wolf say: "You hunters blasted your way across the island, killing everything with fur, feathers or scales. The bison made this land a piss-driven prairie. And, as they declined, we wolves declined and the redskinned ones declined."

"We only wanted the Injuns and wolves to go, not the bison."

"We were all one. We used to have your respect, but now you leave a trail of atrocities. The problem lies in your perception."

"Wolves steal, wolves attack and kill children."

"Sometimes, rarely, starving children that men could not feed or protect. Wolves are a risk, humans are; each is a risk to the other."

"Hundreds of Humans were killed by wolves in Russia."

"How could you tell who killed them? I remember men killing millions of Russians. It was food for us, corpses lying on the ground or hastily buried for food later."

"Wolves kill hundreds of Men in India."

"When small children roam untended, they look like slow deformed deer. Many of them die from hunger. Perhaps a few are killed by some homeless or crippled wolves, but some wolves are not all wolves. One wolf is not all wolves, any more than men are all alike."

"In North America people have been attacked."

"Men try to visit dens and want to play with pups. Bad idea. Biting is only the last defense. Moving dens is preferred."

"Wolves kill children and pets."

"Real wolves or human-raised wolf-dogs?"

"Wolves have to learn to keep to wilderness, to wastelands."

"Wolves go wherever they can eat. Even cities and garbage dumps. Wolves have followed men for generations. Men have followed wolves for generations. The two species act much alike. Hunting deer in groups, making families, defending our territories, and communicating about the weather. How can you fear us when you can see us on the prairie, and you know what we do, and what we are like?"

"Maybe we learned to fear you in the forest, where we could not see you. Forest-dwelling wolves are unseen and more mysterious. I admit, men had a complex spiritual relationship with wolves and other animals for 30,000, no 100,000 years. We drew pictures on cave walls. Made rules, made sacrifices."

"Maybe it was spiritual for you. For us it was social, when to avoid you, when to visit. Wolves are afraid of people and their new weapons for killing wolves." Wolf reared, put his paws on the other's shoulders.

"We feared what you are, what you appear to be."

"The real wolf is hidden, not by its skin, but by the blanket of fear and symbols you clothe us with. Colored in by what you believe. Some Men taught the wolf was evil, not just a symbol of rapacity used to teach lessons, but inherently evil. No wolf is evil. That is just a human category." Their noses were close and warm breath mingled.

"Some primitive tribes believe that all beings are the same and only wear different masks. Apollo, the human god of light, associated with wolves." The Man knew to lean into the wolf and show no fear.

"So why doesn't Apollo protect us, now? And how do you explain the relentless persecution of wolves, ever since man had dumbed down his food on the hoof?" Wolf dropped down, satisfied with the display.

"Apollo is gone, now. We have to protect our animals."

"We have to eat your food because you killed all of ours, the bison, even the deer. But, you killed us because you feared us and could not control us. We have seen you, heard you and smelled you more and more; the human scent is on almost every thing and place."

"But, you have no real value."

"What is the value of a wolf? Enriching nature? Keeping prey healthy and diverse? Economic value from tourism? We have wolf value, like dung beetles have dung beetle value and you have human value."

"Should we worship this value?"

"Like you do money and other symbols? In Japan, the word for wolf was *ookami*, meaning 'great god.' We were beneficial gods because we killed animals that destroyed crops. After the Shoguns lost power, wolves were poisoned by some—at the same time they were revered by others. You men have weak, divided minds."

"I think that you overstate—"

Coyote wondered if he should put in a word for his people, but then the vision faded and he slept.

Coyote leaves his mark

Going fishing Or *Salmon from heaven*

Coyote dreamed of fresh wriggling salmon
and his body took on that movement
pushing Wakanda to the far end of the den.
His mouth watered copiously and Wakanda woke
alarmed, "Coyote, are you mad?"

      "What? No. It is the moon of running salmon.
There will be salmon in the Snake River. I will help
the Nez Perce people to catch them. I am going fishing,
I must go there, now." And he left.

Over the Palouse hills above the Snake river,
he watched the Nez Perce catch salmon
in their weir. He could see the fish leaping.
he could smell the odor of cooking salmon
leaping over the hills to his nose. This was good.
He brushed his fur to look neat and leaped
down the hill.

They welcomed him and said that he could have
all the fish he could catch and carry.
Hunger and greed caused Coyote to take more fish
than was possible to carry. Finally, he lifted the big load
onto his back and began his homeward journey,
after thanking the Nez Perce for their generosity.

Because his load was extra heavy, and he still had
a long way to go, Coyote soon tired.

      "I think I had better rest for a while," he thought.
"A short nap will do me good."

      He stretched himself full length upon the ground,
lying on his stomach, with the pack still on his back.
While Coyote slept, swarms of the Yellowjacket sisters
led by Risa and Tisa dived down and scooped
up his salmon, leaving only bare bones.

Coyote waked very hungry. His first thought was how good
some salmon would taste. Still half-asleep, he turned his head
and took a large bite. To his great surprise and anger,
his mouth was full of fish *bones*! His salmon meat was *gone*!
        Coyote jumped up and down in a rage shouting,
"Who has *stolen* my salmon?! Who has stolen my salmon?!!
The bitches stole my fishes!!! **Wooooo!!!!**"

Coyote searched the ground around him but could not see
any visible tracks. He returned to Nez Perce village
and asked his good friends if he could have more salmon.
    "What happened to you?" they asked when they saw
his pack of bare salmon bones, raising their handsome eyesbrows
and flaring their pierced noses, "Who would dare
to trick the trickiest?"
                    "I was tired and decided to take a nap,"
replied Coyote. "While I slept, someone ate all of the good
salmon meat that you allowed me. I feel foolish to ask, but
may I catch more fish at your dam?"
                        They nodded,
secretly awed at the skills of whomever had done it.

But, the same thing happened again, like an instant replay.
This was more embarrassing than being killed.
                            The third time
leaving, he tripped over Elder Turtle and dropped the salmon.
"Can't you see I'm an important person. I'm FBI. I'm here
to see who is stealing salmon from honest fishers.
You are in the way, so go your way, away, any way
you can! Now! Vamouse! **Scram!**"

Turtle continued to sit there and rest. He watched Coyote
turn red with anger; he watched the Yellowjacket sisters
strip the salmon bones of the delicious flesh in a flash,
behind him, and he watched when Coyote was so stunned that
he stopped his self-important tirade. Coyote fizzled at Turtle
for a moment and ran off in hot pursuit of sisters. Turtle started
after him at a stately pace. Coyote ran fast and dropped

exhausted after a kilometer. The sisters raced on to
the very top of Mt. St. Helen's, far to the northwest.
Turtle plodded along, past the bellowing and blowing
stumbling slowing Coyote.

The sisters entered a hole in the top of the mountain
with their latest load of salmon.

Coyote shouted to Turtle to sit
on top, which he did. Coyote huffed up the slope and filled all the
vents as he went. At the top he started a fire.
When it was smoking, he pushed it under Turtle into the hole,
thinking it would suffocate the Yellowjacket sisters.

Turtle rolled over and his massive shell covered the hole
so no smoke or flames escaped.

Coyote rolled over to rest and breathe, but a rumbling
started deep in the mountain. "Certainly, the sisters are dead
now and we can get the salmon," Coyote said.
The noise became louder and closer to the surface.

Coyote raced down the slope. Even Turtle moved off
the peak just as there was a terrific explosion that spewed
cooked yellowjackets, smoked salmon, fire, rock, and smoke
everywhere. Coyote started wolfing down salmon immediately.
Turtle was taken by the flow down to the river.
Coyote gathered more salmon to carry in his FBI jacket,
as dry, grey ash started to fall. Trees died, animals died,
bees died, people died, but Coyote was fed and had take-home.

Much later, Coyote surveyed other volcanoes. He was still hungry
for salmon. But, there were fewer salmon, now that so many
people liked them. Maybe he could start a fishing company
or a fish farm in the desert. He started south again.

Wolf Envy

"Wolf, wolf, wolf that's all I ever hear about. What's
so good about wolf?" Coyote snarled.
          "Maybe because he doesn't brag, maybe
because he is attentive to his mate, maybe because he's
bigger, in every way, ahem," Wakanda nodded at his sexer.
          "Well, let's just see about that," and Coyote thought,
I will act like a wolf and see what happens.

Early next morning in the crepuscular light, Coyote spotted
a large healthy antelope. He snuck up slowly, jumped out
from behind a tree, and exploded into a furious charge,
but it bounced away.
     Coyote started chasing it, over logs, over hills, overnight.
The next day, Wolf saw a healthy antelope bounce by
and nodded to it. Hours later a sound like a steam engine
reached his ears. Then he saw Coyote puffing up the hill,
"Ahh,huh, ahhh, huh," collapsing on the trail and rolling over,
"ahhh huh, ahhh *huh*."

Wolf thought of killing Coyote, but realized there was no threat
to him. He pissed on the tree nearest Coyote and said,
"Next time, find a weak one, sick or old. You don't have
the sugar or fast-twitch muscles for a quick capture. You only
have fat-powered slow-twitch muscles, like me.
Pick your prey carefully and follow it until it collapses.
Here, chase this stick to practice," and wolf threw
the stick a meter from Coyote.
                    Coyote crawled towards the stick.
     Wolf said, "Practice until you can catch it, Nitwit."
And ran off.
          Coyote rolled over on his back and scratched
his groin. His eyes narrowed. He did not like to be humiliated
in front of trees, especially cedar. He decided to follow Wolf
and spy on him, just as soon as he could breathe.
"Ahh, huuuuhhh."

Coyote saw Wolf running, so he followed at a distance,
but Wolf didn't seem to be chasing anything.

Then Wolf played with his tail, then with a pine cone,
batting it down a hill and chasing it. Coyote was perplexed.
What did all that accomplish?

Later, Coyote witnessed him running
with his brothers and sisters. Still later, Coyote spied on him
with his mate, racing circles around each other, up and down
the hills; then they stopped. He watched them make love
and knot the tie.

Coyote ran home to Wakanda and told her he could make love
like a wolf. He pushed her on the soft moss of their bed
and tried to mount and turn, but they fell apart. Coyote knew
that he could do it, but gave up after ten minutes.

Wakanda said, "That's okay. Maybe there might be a trick to it.
You could ask Wolf," realizing that was the wrong thing to say,
and smiling at the 'coytus interruptus.' Another mistake.

"All I hear is wolf wolf wolf. Maybe you'd just like to run off
with a wolf instead," Coyote said peevishly, "I don't see any
wolf myths around. In fact, I don't see any wolves around.
They were the ones too stupid not to eat poisoned cows,
not me. They were the ones that stopped having pups,
not me. No, I had more pups. More of everything. Coyote means
excess, Coyote means success. I do what coyotes do best."
And he pounced on his mate.

Rancho de Coyo

It was time for vacation again. There was a ban on coyotes
at Mouseworld, so they would have to go up and over
to Montana. Haven't been there for years, thought Coyote.

Along the trail, with Wakanda and grown pups, Coyote thought:
'Getting food was a problem.' There were always plenty of mice,
but it took so long to get a mouthful, much less a stomachful.
        Deer was really good to eat, but, having taught deer to run
to avoid getting killed, Coyote now had a hard time catching
them. The last time he had any luck at all, he was chasing
a deer towards a highway and it got hit by a car—
it was fresh anyway. He popped another mouse.
            So long ago, deer were the only animals on earth
and easy to catch. Maybe he could catch a cow or bull.
        So many in Idaho and Montana.
How could Coyote get ranchers to let him take a few?
Reason with them? Try to steal cows? But, then the ranchers
would get upset and wind up their helicopters.

They saw a nice ranch, set in the valley by a stream,
south of Helena. Wakanda thought 'how beautiful.'
        Coyote thought 'how now.'
"You and the kids bed here for the night, I'll ask the rancher
if we can stay." And he loped off.

He found a dead carcass on the way down and took
something from it. Formed a Clint Eastwood mask. At the house,
he knocked on the door. A middle-aged man answered it.
        Coyote pushed his way in, "I think they might be trying
to kill you," he said. "Have you noticed anything funny about
your stock? Anyone die, get sick, your dog?"
    "My family's up by Missoula, with her mother.
I guess the dog—hey where is the dog?"
        "Listen, it might be poison. I see you're about to eat.
Let me take a few bites first. I have a highly developed sense."
    "Hey, do I know you?" asked Lorn.

"Yea, I'm Jim, live up by the north fork.
We met at, let's see, the Grange last month."

"Well, I guess you're familiar. Sorry Jim, you spooked me."

Coyote sat in the side seat and moved the plate over.
He tried a few bites. "Good, I think I'm on time to help you."

"Here let me get you some, too," said Lorn as he went
to the kitchen.

Coyote freshed up the plate he had eaten
from and moved it back.

"And, we can stay here just like that?" Wakanda asked.

"Well, of course, the poor man died of something. We have
to keep the place running til his family gets back.
It's the neighborly thing to do."

"How'd he die?"

"Hearty attack,
I suspect. Didn't get here in time to help," Coyote sniffed
the body, "Smells like poison."

"Poison, really? Yes, what did you *do*?" she asked.

"Nothing, really, he was just eating his own livestock."

"Did you put something in his food?"

"No, well, just a little flavor from another of his cows."

"And, where was this cow?"

"Back by the hill.
You think it was *bad*?"

"I saw a poisoned bait on my way here."

"That might have been it, but, certainly he could eat whatever
it was; he probably put it there."

"You murdered him?!!"

"Easy, now, no sense in using hate words. I did nothing to him
that he has not tried to do to me for decades. I didn't force
him to eat it."

"You *killed* him!"

"**Enough** woman! He waged
a brutal war to slaughter creature coyotes," Coyote held up
a paw to forestall the accusations he knew would follow,
"as well as the noble wolves, and the imperial eagles,
so his domestic eating-machines would not decline.

116

Think of the wolves, unknowingly eating poison-laced
carcasses, dying in pain, knowing their pups would starve
and the plains would be voiceless. The eagles, no longer
soaring—"
        Wakanda glared, but Coyote continued, as tears
filled his eyes. "So much death. Wolf did not learn, Eagle
did not learn, but coyotes learned. Despite the war, the price
on our heads, we learned, and prospered, and expanded,
making more pups, becoming clever and sneaky, I mean
wisely cautious. We survived, we thrived, and we carried
the flag of the wild, for all those who died.
        "We continued to fire dreams and imaginations, so that
the soul of the west would not die and be lost.
What is the life of some beef farmer compared to
the continuity of Coyote, the icon, the mythic hero,
the triumphant. Let us eat cattle and the cattle will be healthy.
Let us eat sheep and the sheep will benefit and thrive.
Let us eat, now!"
        "Yea, Dad, good going." said Renren.
        Wakanda sat, knowing the deed was done and the
consequences would return to them someday. She knew at least
the pups would be fed for a while.

Cows were really dumb, Coyote thought, standing, chewing
their cuds, dumber than Deer. Nothing distracted them
from food, nothing scared them, why even a woman
could walk up and club one for dinner. What a dilemma!
Should he free the cows to be wild, or eat them?
        Choices, choices. He decided. "Hey magnificent aurochs,
you are in danger. Someone wants to kill you. Quick,
come into the barn. I will *save* you!" So easy,
Coyote thought, as they stampeded to safety.
        As the last one tried to enter, Denny bonked it with
the powerhammer and it collapsed.
        "Fix it up and get ready for dinner," Coyote instructed,
looking over his acquisition.

"Are we cowboys, dad?" Renren asked between bites
at dinner.

Wakanda boffed his head, "Not with food
in your mouth. Were you raised in a hole?"

"Yea!"

"No, we are coybows maybe," Denny said, "other
people are cowbuys, ha, ha."

Coyote was teaching the boys how to lasso, when he saw
the dust in the distance. Not alarmed, he made up a rancher
song, to go with his rancher dance:

"I'm a lone cowhand, from the Rio Grande,
    ain't got no cows, ain't got no hands
    I can see the posse the ranchers are peeved
    So get your mom, it's time to leave.
    Yeehaw! Yeahaowwllll!"

Speed is good Or *Drumming time*

Coyote was rolling down the road in the rancher's den on wheels,
a Winnebago, named after a Native American tribe.
Wakanda looked at him lovingly, although she could not see
his eyes, because of the old Horse blinders she made him wear,
so he could not be distracted by rabbits or anything running
that he could chase.

    "Oh, traveling dog, just a traveling dog,"
he started his road song. Trying to dance on the pedals, however,
just made the van rock and roll, slow and yaw.

  She took off the blinders to stop him, but that was a mistake
as he saw a rabbit. She covered her eyes. They were rolling
now, then not rolling now. 'I guess we are in for the night,'
Wakanda thought. Fortunately, the van rolled to a stop
on a hardpan soil. The family patrolled for mice all night,
then slept.

Jackrabbit watched until he figured Coyote was full. "Hey, there,"
he said. "That thing is pretty fast. If I got one I could be faster?'

  "Why?" asked Coyote, "To catch grass? The grass is not
very fast. Can't you catch it, Rabbit?"

          "Call me Jack. No, I need to run
away from you, plus my running attracts the best females."

  Coyote, lying on his back in the sun, parted his legs
and looked up at Rabbit.

  "It is the way of things," Rabbit expounded, "power
has always shifted from the slow to the fast. It is the fast
that generate interest and wealth. It is the fast—"
Rabbit continued his paean to speed.

  Wakanda rolled over and looked from the top
of the Winnebago at the brainless boisterous males.

  Coyote interrupted and said, "yes, if we all could just go faster."

Wakanda said, "Slow animals are just as successful as fast ones.
Slow wealth, like sunsets and food, is just as good as the fast
wealth of things." She was thoughtful.

Rabbit said that each unit of time saved was more valuable
than the last. People without these things, without this time
would be poor. Turtles and snakes are doomed to backwardness.
"Imagine if we had fleets of these things, these Winnebagos, racing
around the world laden with food and warm wraps, why, why,
it would be utopia. We fast animals would be the nervous system
of the whole planet."

                "Nervous, yes," Wakanda noted, "fever speeds
up our hearts, as much as any excitement. Is it backwardness
to touch the desert, to marvel at opening flowers? To be free
of burdensome things and be happy? Here is the source
of wonder—the sacred, the wild. Your fast things only take us
away from them. Life gets dull. You get dull!

"Things get sterile. We speed away from what is truly valuable,
hoping that speed will provide us with the same meaning
and satisfaction, and we believe that faster is better
and more is more. The soul, cut off, withers and dies,
and we pray that we never stop. We have wealth without touch
and speed without grace. Is that what—"

                The van lurched,
almost tossing her off. Coyote was showing Rabbit how to start
it. Wakanda jumped down and went to check on the pups.

*Dr. Roegrimes: This is what I mean, This is **preposterous**,*
a coyote teaching a rabbit to drive a Winnebago?
Stupid, comic-book shi—

Prof Snootwhistle: You sad whip, I mean really. This is what
I have been talking about, traveling is a fundamental premise of
the coyote cycle. Coyote is always in motion, going nowhere
in particular, along the edge of reality. His movement is associated
with rivers and roads, which can be defined as mythical
boundaries. A river divides the land and offers thresholds for—

Ms. Beangurd: Gentlemen, please, this is the middle of the story,
not to be interrupted lightly; we can address these issues—

Dr. Roegrimes: I will not be throttled or silenced. For too long—

Ms. Beangurd: I'm warning both of you, I can edit this out.

Prof. Snootwhistle: Barnguard, you wouldn't dar—

Coyote wished everything could move fast and go, people,
antelopes, trains, birds, but also seeds and plants. So,
he decided to speed up time. He slipped a drug to Drummer,
the timekeeper of the universe, and it was so.
Drummer speeded up. Everything speeded up.
Coyote was happy. But, later, when he stopped to grab a bite
to eat, he could not catch anything, even a worm,
even a cactus seed. Everything was so much faster that no one
could get anything to eat.

Coyote was hungry. The pups hungry. Wakanda was righteous.
But, then the drug wore off; the drummer slowed,
everything slowed, and was as it was, before Coyote's prank,
sort of, kind of, except for sudden jumps at times.

Later, when everything was almost right again,
driving down the highway, Coyote suddenly saw another
Winnebago coming towards him. As they passed,
Coyote said, "Oh, God." It was another coyote!
    Both vans skidded to a stop.
      Coyote backed up and said, "I'm Coyote, who are you?"
    The stranger said, "You recognized me, but you won't believe
me if I tell you myself."
           "Try me," said Coyote, "I am Coyote, so you
must be younger brother."
           "I think I know a way," said the stranger,
"Let's drive to the next town, and we'll see what the people say.
I'll go first."
      "No, me go first!" shouted Coyote, quickly, sure
that he would be recognized as the original. He drove away.
    The other coyote turned and followed, speeding up.
They drove furiously down the road, Coyote keeping his lead,
mouth open in the window, tasting the air and dry dust of victory.
The town appeared to be racing towards them.

Coyote saw people in the streets. He slowed just a little
so they could see him.

The people were alarmed by the two racing Winnebagos.
In shock they saw the scrawny coyote driving the first one.
"Coyote!" they spoke as one.

And Coyote smiled, knowing he had been recognized.
Then the people saw the driver of the second Winnebago
and breathed, "Oh, God."

Coyote howled and spun out of control
in the dust, banging his head on the steering wheel.

"Now what?" the people asked.

Cultural shock therapy Or *Wealth changes*

It was late morning and Coyote was going home
to sleep. He stopped and grabbed a saguaro cactus fruit
and smeared the black seeds on his front teeth
so he looked toothless. He smeared red organpipe
fruit on his neck and right leg, to look like gore. Then he hobbled
to the den groaning like a tree.

    "What happened?" Wakanda asked when she saw him.
"Were you drinking again?"

        Coyote had been with his mistress
but said, "No, it was Horse, our neigh-bore. We were just grazing
together. I was under him in the shade, eating some grass
to settle my stomach—"

    "Why? Drinking again?"

    "No, I was worried about Renren. But, Horse forgot, thought
I was Wolf, panicked and kicked me over two ridges."

    "Oh, sorry," and her whole stance softened, "let me clean
you up."

    "You're so sweet, really it looks worse than—"
he nuzzled her nose and hurried to curl up, careful to groan
when he lay down.

When he got up in late afternoon, he ate his disguise
and trotted out. "Feel better?" Wakanda asked. "Renren needs
to talk to you," and she handed him the phone.

    "Hi, dad, I'm feeling better. Mom bought me a new
cell phone—"

    "Hmm," Coyote answered.

        "It's great,
she got you one too. Now we can talk more."

  "Hmm, where are you?"

    "Behind you."

        "Ahhh!
you startled me. Why are we talking into boxes, then?"
Coyote asked.

    "Because it's cool."

        Coyote put the phone down

and left to hunt, but first Wakanda gave him his own new phone
to carry on a leg band.

Coyote was hurrying back to his mistress when
the phone rang. Coyote had to stop, pull it out and nail
the speak button.
        "Dad, I'm feeling better, I'm over by
the white sage, waiting for a mouse to volunteer. I was think—"
    Coyote put the phone back in the leg strap. His business
was too urgent for family matters. He decided to pick up
a mouse for Badgera to prime her. As he stood listening
above a likely site, the phone rang again.
              Renren continued,
"I'm feeling good. Playing with Foxy. We're running—"
    Coyote wondered why everyone needed to be in touch
constantly to feed constant reports. He replied honestly:
"I don't want to talk now, talk is for the end of the day, not
for the center of day. Now stop calling me or I'll throttle you."
    "But, dad, you are the one who wants everything to be faster."
    "That was yesterday's Coyote."

Coyote called his mistress, Badgera, with his new phone.
        She continued last night's argument without pause,
"Why aren't you rich, so you can buy me strong scents?"
    "Coyotes are not rich, poets are not rich. It's simple,
I do nothing, and that is priceless. Now, stop calling me at home."
    "But you—" she sputtered. But, I could be rich, Coyote thought,
and have richer, more discrete mistresses.

Just as Coyote reached Badgera's den, the phone rang.
    "Hey dad, can we host an exchange student?" Renren asked.
        "Oh, no. Well—are you still in school?"
        "Seriously, the Predator's school wants to find a host
so we can get an exchange student?"
    "Why are you still living at home? I don't see your brothers;
are they gone?"
        "Dad, mom said we could."
    "Where would this student be coming from? Who are we

sending? We—You? It's you, isn't it!?" the sudden surge of enthusiasm surprised Coyote.

"Yea it's me," Renren smiled coyly.

"And where is the other—"

"Africa."

"Africa?"

"Africa!"

"Where in Africa? And, how in Gila's hind foot are they going to get here? Or you there?"

"Dahomney. There are ways."

"Who—?"

"A real nice guy, Legba."

The young man took off his straw hat, put it on his cane, then sprinkled water on the doorway before he entered, "Greetings to you, honorable sponsor. I am Legba. I am living with you."

"Egbert, welcome."

"Legba."

"Hegbor, welcome."

"Legba."

Coyote sniffed the strange anima, like a coyote, but like an old man with a twisted back and a strange odor. "Do you have a first or last name?"

"Peter Legba. Pleased to meet with you. Renren has told me much of you."

"Please sit," offered Coyote, also pleased that the family would get food and expenses for their guest.

"We have many things in common," Legba noted.

"What?" said Coyote.

Wakanda glared at his bad manners, but said nothing.

"The same birthday in June; the same sign, Mercury in the Sun."

"Oh, how interesting," Wakanda said. "May I offer you a meatpie?"

"Do you have a banana or rice?"

"C'mon!" said Renren, "Some of the girls from school want to sniff you out." And the two left.

That night, Legba gave Coyote an exquisitely wrapped present.

"How, why did you do that?"

"It is a gift, for you."

"But, you could charge cash for that."

"This money, cash, is not the only way to exchange things, you know."

"Yeah, there is stealing, but buying and selling are everything here."

"No, it is a gift, for you, to have, and use."

"You mean I do not have to give anything back?"

"No, not if you don't want. But, now it is a bond between us. You cannot think of that without thinking of me."

"Really, I would not have to think of you."

"No, but it makes me bigger, as it circulates, as you give it away, I travel with it, learning and expanding, and seeing and loving."

"Uh, sure, I was going to sell it or give it away pretty soon."

"Without gifts the wealth dries up, the spirit stagnates and things all start to die."

"I know that. But, it's just a pendant with a scared dog; take it back. Thanks anyway."

"The dog, it is sacred to me."

That night, Coyote admired his money—well, rancher Lorn's money once, but the gift had moved to him—his wealth, his collection of colored paper. He thought maybe he should buy gifts or buy somebody to make and give gifts. There was just as much spirit in money as in other gifts, maybe more. The gift of intensification, of wealth, of worth, the density of symbols of essence, of time. Money is alive, it moves, and changes, starts adventures, like the time … and he fell asleep, as his paws pushed greenbacks.

It was so uncomfortable, like sleeping on bowling balls, that he had to get up. He must be dreaming. The entire den was filled with giant nuts. The money was gone. Renren! Legba! He raced outside, foaming from his mouth— "***Aaahhhhhh!!***"

Legba had changed the money to Mongongo nuts, his own African currency of wealth, and then gone to school with Renren, who wore the pendant with pride.

Wet behind the ears Or Volunteers at sea

Coyote was blind with rage, still, plotting his revenge, but Legba
and Renren seemed to have vanished. Wilderness school, Wakanda
had said. He was going to have to recoup his fortune from
the other animals, unless he could sell them those ridiculous nuts.

"What can we do!?" Ant shouted at the weekly meeting of CVA
(Coyote Victims Anonymous). "He ruins everything he touches,
unbalances every life, shorts every circuit—*ah*!"
        "We have to send him somewhere. Listen I have an idea,
we could draft him in the army," suggested Peccary.
                        "Wait! Or enlist him in the Peace Corps."
            "Yea, tell him it's a vacation to a tropical island," added
Stinkbeetle.
                "I'm going to make the call now. I'll disguise myself
as Coyote, then—"
                    "How will you do that?" Stinkbeetle asked Peccary.
                        "This old moth-eaten carpet for fur, pizza
slices for ears and a wet eraser for a nose. Should work."
        "And, where will you do this?" asked Groundsquirrel.
        "Phoenix should have a Peace Corps office."
    "Well, I guess it's settled. I propose a toast to the time we
can wave good-bye to that proud pisser and egotistical airhead."
        "Hear, hear," cheered Ant and the others.

Coyote wasn't sure how it happened. The vacation flight
from Phoenix had a large holiday group going to some
South Pacific island. Strange group. They were acting like he
was their brother and he would be with them for years.
Must have something to do with the massive paperwork
he had had to sign. He settled into the seat.

"Hi there! My name is Pete. I am here to orientate you before
we land, before we are divided up and put to work," the slim banker-
dressed guy paused, "The Polynesian islands of Tuvalu stretch across
the ocean for 805 kilometers from Samoa.
        It is one of the world's smallest and lowest countries

and one of the least developed. The main island,
Funafuti, is the capital. With the other eight islands or atolls,
with its beaches, lagoons and palm trees, it is one of the last
unspoiled paradises in the Pacific. No rats, no coyotes.
The traditional way of life on its more remote islands is
untouched by the modern world. The history of Tuvalu goes
back over 5000 years and is a fascinating and unique blend
of myths, folklore and reality. We need to help preserve it."

Coyote listened intently: "Blah, blah, blah, Tutti-frutti, mumble,
mumble mumble, beaches, drone, drone, no coyotes, blah—"
No coyotes! What was going on here? Except for humans,
or rats and fleas, coyotes were the most adaptable forms of life
on the planet. No coyotes? Not likely.

"What island are you going to?" asked the young—very young,
smooth and unblemished, Coyote noted—woman sitting next
to him, "I'm assigned to Nanumaga!"
                          Coyote lowered his eyes and looked
at her plump lap. In one hand she held a roll of toilet paper;
in the other a bottle of hand sanitizer.
                          She followed his gaze
and asked, "Did you get your TP?"
                          Coyote looked at her plump lips.
        She grabbed his ticket and said, "Nukulaelae. Wow!
That should be fun," She dabbed his drooling chin with her
TP roll, "We can visit during the semi-annual volunteer fests—
Oh!" as Coyote squeezed a plump breast and she said,
"You wanted the toilet paper again? I'm Tiffany."
        Coyote held the TP under his chin for a moment
and had an epiphany.

Pete was finishing up, "—peaceful atmosphere and the palm-
fringed beaches. Pandanus, papaya, banana, breadfruit, pulaka, and
coconut palms are typical. *Fafetai!* Which means thank you."
        The planeload of volunteers clapped enthusiastically.

"No coyote myths?" Coyote asked.

"No, of course not.
How would they get here? Swim?" Steve asked. "No,
the native myths are all about birds and fish. For instance,
the story of Eel and Flounder—"

"Animal house?" Coyote asked.

Steve frowned, "Not funny. The Eel and the Flounder
were great friends, sharing things in the sea. One day they
decided to test who was stronger by carrying a huge stone.
Eel picked it up to carry, but they were arguing so viciously
that Eel dropped the stone on Flounder who was almost
crushed and became very flat.

"When he got free, Flounder hit Eel hard in the stomach.
As Eel ran for his life he started vomiting from the blow.
He kept vomiting and his body became thinner and thinner—"

"How could he run?" Coyote asked. "They were under
water."

"No. There was no water then. After hiding, Eel went back
to the stone, which was black, white and blue. He threw
it high in the air, but part of it stuck—

"What if there were Coyotes, but they were invisible?"

"Oh, I give up! Anyway, parts of the stone became
the sky, night, day, and water—"

"But, there were just three colors," Coyote noticed.
"How, could—"

But, Steve had turned to Sarah a slim brunette
from Oregon. Coyote looked at Sarah and the drool started
forming.

Tiffany explained that the three goals of the Peace Corps
had to be kept in mind at all times: "To learn about the foreign
culture, to teach about American culture, and to work together
on the problems at hand."

Coyote's mind just did not have room
for three more rules, although it had room for parts of her.

Tiffany scolded him, "This is serious. Get your paw off me.
The islands are sinking."

"Why?" Coyote asked.

"Because the sea level is rising."

"Why?"

"Because the ice caps are melting."

"Why?" Coyote continued.

"Because of global warming."

"Why" Coyote asked once more.

"Because of greenhouse gases that we make and release."

'Release' Coyote thought and moved closer.

"Seriously. These islands could disappear in our lifetime."

"No, I mean, why can't I paw you?"

"Because, I have to save these islands and their people. The rising salt water will spill inland and ruin crops and gardens."

Coyote said, "You're right. Tell me more," and he put his head on her lap.

She twoggled his ears absently and continued: "As the ocean rises, the land will be submerged more often by storms …"

"It isn't just about sex," Coyote explained, "it's the teaching of sex, I mean love and sharing, cultural exchange."

"No," Tiffany said, "we are from the same culture."

"No," said Coyote, "I am from a neglected minority, native americans."

"Are you a Native American?" Tiffany asked. And she petted Coyote's head.

After much more petting and the inclusion of many more body parts, Coyote shared with her the meaning of his name: "Coy means shy or innocent, and 'ote' is a suffix referring to other. So, you see. I am just an innocent other." And, he caressed her breast again and put his head on her lap. He thought: 'Land was the problem. Easy fix.' Coyote had made land once—a distant memory. 'There had to be a way to try to add land to keep it from rising seas from global warming. Maybe, if—'

"C'mon, my little coyscout, time to deplane and save the earth." Tiffany lead him by the nose into the light. But, then he was separated from his new conquest and sent to a different island with a different volunteer.

Day one: Sunburn. Day two: Sick from drinking water.
Day three: Crabs from another volunteer. Day four: Fleas
from another animal. Day five: Roast rat for dinner.
Day six: Swim to freedom. Day seven: Rest, to recover from
drowning. Trickster or trickee?—was there a perverse
status change involved?

Eventually, Coyote started working with the volunteers.
They were all hard-working and earnest, if slightly idealistic,
people, easy to trick, easy to bed, hard to ignore, and hard
to escape. With Amber and four locals, he relocated a well
over the meniscus of fresh water. He did not understand
Amber, who ignored him except when she had to scratch an itch
with him. The work was boring and hot. The natives
had a tendency to evaporate in the afternoon. Smart natives.
Coyote started to emulate them, risking the ire of Amber,
who was dedicated to the three Corps rules.

Coyote gave birth to a new escape plan a mere three months later.
It was the same plan from the sixth day. Swim for it. But, this time
he went with the outgoing wave. He floated on a rubber duck
for days. Then a miracle. A white ship, the Hospital Ship
Polynesian Hope, picked him up. Doctors without Boarders?
        'Not any more,' Coyote thought.

Doctor Canis Or *What's not to lick*

The first explorer looked through a wilderness of trees, what old loggers called doghair, hard to walk through. The others followed, stopping to dig into the fertile soil, the flesh of this new planet. But, suddenly sharp shovels came over the horizon and decimated their fellows. They struggled on, under constant attack. Some of the furrows proved to be good hiding places and many survived the violent onslaught.

Coyote couldn't stand the itching. The tide had turned; the fleas had got him. And, these were Arizona fleas. He had felt so good after getting off the ship in Los Angeles and hitching back home. Must have been the inviting tenderness of his skin. He had to find his medicine bag. Fortunately, it was still on the Manabozho tree where he had abandoned it years before. He put some powder in a rolled up piece of bark and blew it on his torturous guests.

After four weeks on a medical ship, Coyote decided that he could cure anything. So, he went directly to the University of Phoenix Medical Center in Scottsdale. He found a white coat and put it on. Stethoscope, check. Clipboard, check. Serious expression, check. He was a Doctor. Now to find some patients.

Patients were more rare than Doctors at this hospital. Then he heard the voice of authority: "Excuse me Doctor, you know the rules for badges?"

Coyote turned slowly and said archly, "May I help you?"

"Yes, I'm Doctor Humphill. I was reminding you of the badge req. Sorry. Are you new here? What's your specialty?"

"I am a sialipractor. I practice the science of restoring health through a special manipulation of nerve function."

"And, exactly how do you do that?" asked Dr. Humphill superciliously.

"Stomatoniption, exactly."

"Hmm, yes, I see."

"It is of course a rare specialty. I am always afraid that I will dry up, but fortunately I have zythology to fall back on."

132

"Very impressive, I must say, I was tempted to enter that area myself at Harvard. Did I see you there?"

"Oxford, ektually, although I interned at Columbia. Well, let me see your tongue, Doctor. Ahh, thank you. And, what is your specialty now, if I might ask?"

"Oh, just plain old vanilla neurology, heh, heh."

"Well, if I find a case that merits your attention, I will certainly call on your expertise." Coyote walked off, adjusting the Richard Chamberlain mask.

"Ah, nurse Caudel, how are you?" The canny doctor asked.

"I've been asked to help you Doctor, with the lady patients."

"Oh, really. I suppose that would put them more at ease, although I haven't had any complaints, yet."

"Could you explain your procedures to me. I had no time to prep."

"Well, it's a manipulative, body-based method applied with movement, moisturization, and added warmth on sensitive neuropheric body parts."

"Oh, tee-hee, sounds like you're going to lick them back to health."

"If it works."

"Doctor Humphill mentioned your work in zythology. I am not familiar—?"

"It's the study of beer. All human civilizations are based on beer or ale. Why do you think agriculture took off? Hey, inebriation on call."

"Seriously?"

"As serious as I am about my stomatoniption."

"What does that mean?"

"It means tongue-washing in Latin, part of my work as a sialipractor."

"You do—you lick them?"

"It gets results. Medicine is an art."

"I'll be right back. I just think you should wait for me, before you see Mrs. Ditherwin," and she walked off.

Coyote ignored her. "Patient 6071. How are you today?"

"Am I just a number to you Doctor?"

"Yes, in health care, all people are numbers, including the staff; so yes, you are just a number. It could be worse, remember, for educators you are an empty jug, for stores you are a consumer, to your family you are a money machine, and to bacteria you are just meat. So, count your blessing, number 6071. How are you feeling?"

"Bad enough to be in a hospital."

"What seems to be the problem."

"Shouldn't we wait for the nurse?"

"If you wish, she had to run for a moment. There's the camera."

"Oh, I trust you. Must be those puppy-dog eyes," Mrs. Ditherwin flirted. "It's just that I am so tired. I was worried it was cancer or Atkinson's or something. I have a skin rash. My neck hurts, and I'm depressed. My sons never visit."

"Well, let's look at you. Could you put your elbows on the table, please? There."

"That was quite nice. It's about time you Doctors used skin-temperature instruments. What did you use? I didn't see it."

"Trade secret, I'm afraid. I want you to get up on the table and lie on your side, and I'll swab that skin."

"That is so relaxing. Is that a special chemical? I could sleep."

"No, it's a glossoscope, just an updating of an ancient technique used by the O'odham."

"Are you Irish, dear?"

"No, let me work," and Coyote primed and employed the glossoscope. "Well, I can taste—tell that you need to reduce your sodium, and increase potassium and calcium. A soy drink would work. As for the skin, just lick—lotion it everyday with a good oil. To relax before bed, I recommend you lick—lie down and meditate. Think of mice—millions of waves and just drift into sleep. I think you will be fine. You are healthy, so don't—"

"Time's *up*, imposter!" Dr. Humphill charged, "Guards, take this man out and hold him until the police get here. Mrs. Ditherwin, I hope you were not—"

But Mrs. Ditherwin had fainted.

"You raped that woman with your tongue," Nurse Caudel said.

Coyote explained: "I try to establish harmony
between the body and the spirit, and saliva is the bond
that connects the two with its fluid form. Results are results,
less is more—" The guards dragged him off.

"Oh, Doctor Humphill, will she be okay?" Nurse Caudel asked.

Humphill replied: "I guess; she's smiling. You know,
I never trusted that new guy. He simply was not writing enough
script. Our sponsor Drug companies would have been upset."

"No one will be sorry to see the last of the likes of him."

"I like that new Doctor," Mrs. Ditherwin said, "He was honest
and warm. Will he be back next week?"

"Let me get this call," Coyote said.

"Sure, buddy," said the man in blue,
"but I ain't taking no handcuffs off."

Coyote nodded as he opened the phone. "Yes? Oh, no.
No, Renren, daddy is not a psychopath; he's a naturopath.
No, it's not sex therapy, it's Canitherapy. Now, where is Legba?
Remember, some predators eat their young."

"Where is the perp? Shit, get *after* him!"

"I don't know, escaped somehow. Let's get moving. I'll drive."

"Don't hit that mutt. Watch that dumpster. There, turn
right. I see a white coat."

It took Dr. Humphill took three hours to
explain that he did not look like the 'perp.'

Getting a meassage

New York—nothing like his last trip here, for love and wealth.
This time—ah, best not dwell on it—the new gods would help
him find Legba and get back his riches—
Here was a good alley to piss, then start the search. He
approached the wall.
   "Hey, look, it's a wolf!" a boy's head said from a dumpster.
            'What? Wolf?'—That got coyote's attention.
        "No, it's just a fox. Look how scrawny and short it is."
    "Who cares. Let's have some fun with it," Waldo said,
throwing a lump of asphalt and hitting the raised rear leg.
        "Here's a brick—hey, what's that shadow?"
    "Come on, it's just a cheap movie effect, it's—"

Flashback— *(or in writing, like now, a parback)*
It felt so good to sleep, coyote thought, and rolled
over. It's just that he was so weak, he could barely
lift his snout to see if there was food in sight. **Wufff.**
No, no chips, no mice. He fell asleep.
                                    Later
as he crawled out of the den, he saw a familiar
flickering light by the pups' den. The pups
were sprawled in front of the new television.
"It's evening," he growled, "cool, time for hunting,"
and with that he collapsed next to them.
Coyote said, "I made that box you know,
so kids would like me."
                        "Yea sure, dad."
And that's what set him off to thinking.
Something was wrong. There must be a reason
he was so weak. People were not thinking of him,
not wondering or admiring his exploits—why?
It seemed there were new gods being worshiped
and coyote had to know why.
Coyote was nothing if not cutting edge
So he decided, New York. —End of disjointed narrative.

Coyote was reading the paper at *The Deposit Box*,
a small breakfast nook by Central Park, enjoying
his first coffee in a year, contemplating *The Post*
headline: "Honor students ripped apart and eaten
by mad dogs—" Dogs? Crap, what was wrong with this paper?
For that matter, with forensic science? Dogs? Please.
He was going to have to correct this. Not fox, not dog,
this was coyote violence, a noble response to
the depredations of some terrorist youth.
He looked back to the inside page of the paper
and got the address of the paper. Time to correct
this injustice before it got pushed to page eight.

The building was certainly impressive enough.
He couldn't even see the top from the sidewalk
and his neck hurt from trying. Sometimes he wished
he could fly like Buzzard. Clutching the newspaper
he strode boldly into the lobby, aiming directly for
the north elevators to the top. Best to start
at the top.

After a maze of changes and having to provide
inducement for the operator of the last elevator
to take him, he arrived in a marble foyer, sighed,
and watered a large banana tree in a pot,
and spit out a small piece of pin-striped wool flannel.

He paused, suddenly a center of quiet in a hurley
mass of bustle, sniffing the cooled air, observing
the threads of power and where they went.
He moved slowly with cautious dignity
or the beginnings of arthritis or lumbago.

Doors opened. An amplified voice greeted him:
"Come in, little legend, I watched you arrive."
There in the studio, a giant visible den, enthroned
in a sound room, waited on by minions of speakers
and readers, was Media, the Initiate of Information,

Displayer of Data, Facilitator of Facts, Massager of Memes,
and Wonk of Wisdom.

"I am so pleased to be in here," Coyote said.
    "You are already inside me," said Media. "Everything you do
is in me. But, you don't do much, now. You live in stories.
Stories are dying. It's all news and reality. Actors, amateurs,
politicians, wealthy dilettantes—Its all the same now,
and they all worship me, so beat off," Media said, nodding
at a cute pneumatic girl carrying a data cube.

"But, stories are dying," Coyote keened, "the god,
Satellitedish, just dishes out the same stuff to the world.
Only one person tells everyone! And, they do not tell
my history or Beaver's stories or Eagle's. What is
this monopoly? Yours are just general stories, sanitized,
pablumized, monotonized, for everyone. Can you
tell a story? *Try*! Really, I'm listening." Coyote rotated his ears.

"Well, okay, sure, I know stories: Two blondes, one
on each side of the street—details at eleven!
    "Hey listen, bandless pup, you don't have market
share—oh, sure, you're amusing, but this is
Saturday morning filler entertainment kid stuff.
You want airtime for those snotty stories, go see
Spurdock, the demi-god of fast-food news.
            Really kid, you're bothering me. Make-up!"

Coyote sat still, "Listen, why not work together.
I could have my own teevee Show. What could
we call it? *Life: Starring: Coyote*! It could be a detective
doctor series with that double-d actress—"
        "No, that would never work, you're an animal. No one
wants to hear you—they want to see you water-ski
or do a stupid pet trick, walk around with a trashcan
on your head, bite a fat person, get it?"
                        "I know that! I mean
younger brother coyote is an animal. Know? No, that's it!

I could be a fake-crash, deserted-island survivor!
       "I coyote, am the ultimate survivor, and I could use
the trip to an island paradise, look at my fur, tangled,
tarry. I need to get away."

"You're history, pal. Old hat, moldy myth, soiled suds,
you can't even be updated with a Mohawk
and a make-over. Just retire gracefully and enjoy
your declining years—here's a day pass to
Opra and Scrubs. Go wild, fuzzbutt.
       "Refreshment please. Ah, thank you so much, dear."
All of Media's other hundred arms were pointing at feeds.

Coyote was not happy at being dissed
or dismissed. As he slunk from the corridors
of power he entered another narrative warp:
In the old days, of mud and digging sticks,
Coyote impersonated the Creator, making humans
out of mud and then buffalo, elk, deer, antelope and bear.
Now, he could make people out of computers and wires,
if he had to. They would do his bidding, watch him
and worship him. Maybe later, if it came to that.

Coyote remembered the gigantic, people-swallowing
monster he had once defeated by cunning, by cutting
out pieces of the giant's flesh from inside to feed himself
and the other prisoners—those were the days, those
people worshiped him, because he was smarter;
they hung on every word he said, did everything
they could to honor him. Now—now, the people-eating
monsters are corporations and political cows—
how could he defeat them? There was no flesh to cut,
just laws and profits. Hmm. Profits, Coyote smiled.
Take away Media's power and he could not profit
and who would worship a dark impotent lump?

Coyote finished pissing on the junction boxes
and admired the sparks and hissing smoke.

That had felt really good. Every god had feet of clay
and coyote had enough piss to make mud
puddles under every god. Media could be fixed
but coyote could always drink more and reaffirm
his power and might. Maybe there would be compromise,
maybe all out war.

"I never thought of that," Media said in Coyote's imagination.
"You're not as smart as I am," said Coyote in his imagination.
"Look at me," exclaimed Anchorman, "I'm a talking head."
"And so you shall always be, and everything you say will be
updated and made old at the next update, and you will be
forgotten, except as a famous face," Coyote smirked. Imagination!
The talking head echoed the word, *"famous!"*

But, fame didn't fill your stomach and an army of one
travels on its stomach after all, which is why things were
so slow unless you used your legs, too.
Between mouthfuls of waffles, Coyote knew he had
to convince the other gods that he was one of them,
that he still had IT (Imagination Techniques).

Visiting the NY temple of the new young gods

Outside in the alley, he saw a man with a ridiculous mane
emerge from a golden dumpster. "Are you a god?"
Coyote asked.
       "You know me, I am *famous*," said
Forest Trump, the entrepreneur and hotel impresario.
     "Yes," nodded Coyote, "and where do the other
new gods live?"
       Forest looked down the alley, "In that
crumby low building, over there, in the shadow of mine."
   Coyote started walking there and heard the trumpster
say, "Wait, I can tell you how to get rich like me."
     But, Coyote was focused on his destination.
  A faint echo followed him: "You're mired! No, you're wired!"
    It was a low building in stone, little glass, very
traditional wall street bunker. Coyote went in, as the door
was held open. He walked down the hall, nails clicking
on the floor. There in the pantheon of industry and profit,
each on a marble pedestal, stood living images of the new gods:
Shortermprofit, Bottomline, Inflation, Growth, Progress,
Loser-worker, Welfare, Wildlife, Sports, Fashion, Sales,
Collateraldamage—and there on the center throne,
most important of all, Humanity.
   Coyote noticed the trend, and he addressed Wildlife first,
"Oh, great nature god—"
        "—Oh, no, wrong god, more denatured,
really, like alcohol. Sorry, I'm just a party-god, a fraternity
version of Dionysius. Party on, pupitudinous pal!"

"Oh, god," Coyote thought, this was not going to end well.
He gazed at them. Bottomline, sharp and hard like scissors
that cut off everything above it, a full-mad half-Procrustes
fitting everything to his small iron bed. Loser-worker
proclaiming through tears that souls and spirits were
so much bigger and more important than Success. Sports,
hulking underneath layers of protection, tried to form
an opinion, or even a sentence, troubled by bloated salaries

and coddled players. Fashion stood, sucking in her
cheeks to look thinner, while pulling her forehead tight
and making sure her image reflected well from any
smooth surface. Sales looked hard at Coyote,
assessing his net worth and potential to pay, said,
"You're going to need a new pelt there, better clothes—"
        "What?" said Fashion, realizing it was not about her
and cooing, "Oh."
                        Sales continued, "—it's about image.
You need to scream sophistication, embody *power!*"
    "Powuh?" said Sports, flexing a bicep.
                                    Progress snorted,
"This is the old nature, no genetic improvement,
probably infested with fleas, not toilet-trained. Ignore him."
        Coyote tried to make eye-contact with Welfare,
who just sighed, as Collateraldamage just lifted
a thumb towards the exit. Coyote started to slink,
but, his eyes were drawn to Humanity, the greatest
of the gods with the greatest generation, and the greatest
appetite, sitting like a living black hole, drawing all
into itself, converting all flesh into human flesh—
on the event horizon, coyote could see a million
tiny individual faces with open mouths and clutching
fingers, frozen on the surface limits—

Coyote backed away and started a self-importance dance:
"The trickster is the hero of uncertainty, the lover of ambiguity,
the creator of new ideas. Let us honor me, umm the trackster,
shower him with food and luxuries." He shouted:
"Let the paleolithic legend *live* again!"

Praising himself, Coyote grew stronger. He knew he could
not defeat these gods quickly. It had taken thousands of years
for things to change to this, and it might take thousands
more to get better, if there was time, if Humanity did
not eat everything first.

Hurricane Pompadour

Coyote had noticed that two bases had been empty, Weather and Death. He wondered where they were. Then, outside, he encountered Weather. "What happened to Nature?"

"Demoted," was the answer. "Left for dead, unappreciated. She suggested I go out on my own, so, sigh, I did. Now I have the attention, the television exposure."

"You know, I have always been a huge fan, you're everywhere, working and keeping things moving, making life interesting."

"Why thank you," blushed Weather, pulling a cloud over her face.

Coyote said, "I have few sheephead's fish on a beach down in Florida, I was wondering if you could help me wash them?"

"Florida, well sure, it's a little late in the season for a hurricane, but I think I can accommodate a friend."

"Also, I have a few buildings in NY that need a really hard pressure wash."

"Sure, it can be the same storm. You'd be amazed at how I can renew them. Watch this."

"This is Newsflab Eight with breaking news. Hurricane Pompadour formed suddenly in the Carrybean and is pounding on the Keys. The path could intromit the Gulf or Atlantic or somewhere in between. Our Weather Expert, Dr. Charley Teller explains how this unseasonable—"

Coyote was standing on the street watching a window of nine television sets multiply the drek. He started the long trek back to Arizona. There he would wait until his name was as revered as the other gods and the people begged for his guidance and wisdom.

NewsrudeNine presented its program on rabid dogs making the streets unsafe. Then newsreader Harvey Barnswallow reported that Hurricane Pompadour was beating a direct path north to New York.

Other Blooms Or *What's a woman to do*

Months later, Coyote sat propped up in his chair, eyes staring,
mind empty, waiting for inspiration to fill it, so that he could
express it and become a great leader—
        "The pups are starving,
there are no cattle to feed them. I cannot find enough roots.
Can you not help me?" Wakanda asked.
        "What? How *dare* you!"
Coyote erupted in rage. "Never address me in that fashion!
I am no common drone, no working stiff, no brainless twit,
no little git, to be spoken to thus by a *woman*. Tomorrow,
I'll be great, *known*, respected for my words of wisdom.
What pups?"
     "How, oh how, could you forget?" she remanded.
 "I will crush my enemies with the weight of my reputation,
I will have so many women, I will not need you, too old
to be a consort with greatness, too ugly to be the wife
of a great warrior-poet, the *leader* of humanity, as I will be!"
Coyote shouted. "Bring me something to eat and drink."
    "Will dirt be enough and some urine?" Wakanda
asked softly and sweetly. But Coyote had already refocused
on the spot which would be the doorway to his greatness.
Wakanda exited the door of the den, the door to
the first world.

Wakanda fed her children, then taught them how to hunt,
not just for garbage but for wild animals.
  She thought to herself: Males? Why are they the ones
to forsake food for Perfection? Or to have to be the tricksters
or troublemakers? Cannot females do anything males can do?
She put her masks in order.

What is this next world? Wakanda wondered. Just
the underworld of the dead, so much dirt and darkness?
  Was it the dimension of imagination, where she was borne
by light and clouds? Was it just the realm of what
was denied or forbidden, what could not be obtained or held?

The world of plants? Of humans? Where coyotes
were half-way between, and denied both realms?
She toyed with a blue Palo Verde blossom.
Suddenly, she passed within it—

Joy and laughter Or To the Fortress of Duplicity

Coyote heard them long before he saw them. At first
the sound of a helicopter gave him pause, as he remembered
the famous battle of the desert with Colonel Cornpen
for the survival of all coyotes. Then it landed; others followed.

"Please prepare for the arrival of *Media*," bawled
the safari-suited functionary.

Media exclaimed: "How can any
one *live* in these conditions."

"This is my working environment,"
Coyote noted haughtily.

"No. fool, I mean *me*! Reduced to one
feed, one camera. I am almost blind."

"Turn this way, Sir." The cameraman directed, "light's better."

And Media turned from coyote to the exoskeleton
standing by the wall.

Coyote hurried to stand next to it.
"I knew you would come for me."

"Fashion is outside, too.
Thought the air would invigorate her skin." Media announced.

Coyote began the steps of a royal acceptance dance,
saying, "I knew that you gods needed a new leader, someone

with the vision to unite all theft, I mean, life, someone with
the charisma to command the fealty of other looters, I mean,
leaders, someone with the balls to insem—I mean inspire,
the women of the world to take their proper places.
I Coyote am ready to earn your respect and trust
and am willing to serve—excuse me—"
and Coyote had to shuffle to follow the cameraman,
who was filming the exoskeleton, as Media examined it.

   "Just a souvenir of an old unpleasantry. Let me give it
to you as a memento of my victory," Coyote offered.

     "Victory?" said Media, archly, "Yes, of course,
and your people need you more now, and your gods need
your wisdom," Media recovered smoothly, then gestured
to the half-mortal Gofor, "Kleenex, thank you. It is quite musky
down here. Come, we shall adjourn topside," and left.

  Coyote tried to keep his dignity but had to scramble to try
to keep between Media and the camera, which was off anyway.

By the entrance of the den, posed by the tree, with one hand
on the bark and her other shading her eyes, was Fashion.
The cameraman went first and set up, checked conditions
and pressed buttons. Media and Coyote emerged and strode
to Fashion, Coyote trying to slow down. He thought
that she would make a good consort.

       As he leaned to buss
her cheek, she gestured to Make-up, who intercepted
Coyote and dusted him with something that smelled
like flea-powder and pancake flour. "There," she said sweetly,
"now your nose won't be shiny." Coyote looked like he had
been snuffling after mice in the sand. She added: "Don't touch
mistress" —Coyotes ears went to full alert at the word—
"simply 'mou' the space an inch from her perfect cheek,"
And, she pinched Coyote's butt and winked.

     Coyote thought he could certainly make room
for her in his heroic harem of harlots.

Fashion was tapping her toe impatiently. Media was looking
at his watch and listening to the Middle East feed.

The cameraman was checking the light. The assistants
were spaced around Fashion like crows around a biscuit,
one after the other darting forward to repair
some microscopic damage. Coyote was dampening the sand
with his medicinal saliva, doubtless curing the ailments
of hundreds of fleas.

Media gestured to Gofor, who ran
to the helicopter. Coyote ran over immediately and asked,
"Is he going for my crown and cape?"

Media looked amused,
"Capes are for comic-book characters. Your mantle
and laurel are in your Fortress of Solitude, with your scepter
and warrants of authority. I have sent for the helicopter."

"Will I have a jet?"

"Air Farce One."

"Mansion?"

"A stronghold."

"Servants?"

"Sentries."

"Armored Limousines?"

"Armed conveyances."

And, Media turned to the arriving helicopter. Coyote waited
as befit an important—no, supreme—deity, thinking
that he had to ask for some jewels and gardens.
Assistants swarmed around Coyote, buzzing with activity,
escorting him first up the double steps of the Dell helicopter.
Then ushered Media and Fashion.

Coyote stated, "Titles, there
must be decent titles."

"Master of the Multiverse?" said Media.

As the bird lifted off, Coyote watched the assistants head
towards a line of buses with three large letters on the side,
but he couldn't read them, except the 'C' maybe.

After an hour, Coyote looked down and saw ramshackle
houses of tin and cardboard in a dry gulch, a few figures
moving listlessly, and several not moving at all. "Media, be
a sweetie and ask the pilot to cross a cleaner part

of the desert?"

"Coyote, these are your people. They are poor
and suffering under the yoke of Globalism. They need help,
your help."

"Nonsense, there have always been poor.
There will always be poor. They are the meat of the earth,"
and he smiled at Fashion, "I'm sure they can bear a few
more taxes to help me. There is nothing I can do, except to
be an example, a Figure of Importance that they can joy in."
The bird flew over a smoking dump, being sorted through
by people in rags. "Oh, look," Coyote exclaimed, excitedly,
"something shiny," pointing at the horizon.

"That would be your Fortress," drolled Fashion.

As they approached, Coyote was disappointed by how harsh
and dilapidated it looked. Then he understood: "How clever
to make it look run-down and grim. That barbwire
is an excellent touch. Who would break into that and steal
my riches? Those guards? Are they retainers in disguise?"

"As always, sir, your ability to see right through us is nothing
short of amazing. We're going to land on that pad, now."
After a smooth landing Coyote was escorted through
the main building. "*Wow!* This disguise is thorough.
When do things change?"

"Very soon." Media shrugged.
Coyote noticed that the walls now were painted and stronger
looking. He figured his quarters would be a golden oasis.
They approached a wagon painted like a circus wagon, with the
large letters, CVA.

Coyote was enchanted. "My own show?"

"For no one else!" said Gofor.

"What does it stand for? Coyote Virgin Ass—?"
As Coyote peeked in, he felt a firm push from behind.
"Don't, I command!" and whirled around in the barred trap.

Gofor was smiling at him. His face slowly darkened
and became more handsome— "Legba!"

"You got my *name* right!" exclaimed
Legba, "and this circus here, it is so *you*! So 15-minutes ago!"

Coyote reached into his bag and took out a mouse mask. He put it on and started to escape, but the bars became hardware cloth. He quickly put on a mosquito mask, but the metal became a fine screen.

"*Dammit!*" Coyote shouted, throwing down the masks. "Fashion, turn the *key!*"

Fashion grabbed the key but put it in her purse. Her face coarsened a bit.

"Renren?" Coyote groaned. "For Spirit's sake, let me out of here. This is not funny anymore. Don't make me *eat* you!" Coyote gazed as the wagon adjusted and the screen became bars again. He tried to squeeze through but the bars narrowed. 'What kind of thing is this?' he wondered.

"It's an invention of mine," said Media, who came close and held his hand, "it reads you and responds in the opposite way."

"Ha, so all I have to do is want to stay," Coyote closed his eyes and accepted his imprisonment. Slowly the circus wagon transformed itself to a cardboard hut. Coyote ran at the door but bounced back. He howled in frustration.

"Did I mention that the wagon has a sense of humor, too?" said Media, tossing his hair and spreading his hands.

Coyote snuffled, "You are making a mistake. When she hears of this, Wakanda will trick you flat so badly that you won't know who you are for a hundred years."

"Is she that good?" Media asked softly.

"Yes, she could do anything—" and Coyote looked closely at Media. "Oh, shit. *Et tu*, bitch?"

Legba and Renren left discretely.

The Media mask dissolved, and Wakanda stood before him, more radiant and vital than Fashion, more powerful than Media, more comprehensive than Humanity.

Coyote was confused, "Whyyy?"

"You *fool*! My husband, the wily fool, the useless **tool**,
the dimwit who sits by the door to other realities and uses
his 10-watt wit to separate the half-wits from their little riches,
to profit from ignorance or suffering. A charming smiler who
steals money and hearts, but cannot recognize the true
value of either, a crafty con-artist who knows how to work
the closing door, who knows how to shrink things,
to unjoin them and take them apart like a silly scientist
of the mechanical dream.

      —But, you don't know, and you never
imagine that the door opens as well, that whatever can be taken
apart can be made whole, that the door is a necessary part—"

"Will I ever get out of here?"

"Of course. I am not cruel. When you can understand
the way of wild nature; when you can be humble, poor
and powerless, the door will open." She pulled his dry nose
through the bars and bussed it with her lips.

And she took off her Wakanda mask and there was nothing
underneath, and the mask fluttered to the ground,
and Coyote heard the fading sounds of gentle
laughter and soft paws.

Three Perspires

Prof. Snootwhistle: "To continue our argument, Coyote doesn't just relate to the river. He IS the river, He's traveling in its banks—"

Dr. Roegrimes: "Rubbish, he has no control over the river or its violent current or impossible crossings. You are just trying to defend these idiot stories about a dog driving a Winnebago. Nothing—"

Prof. Snootwhistle: "Symbolically, nonmedical Doctor of typing or kiddie lit, heh, heh, Coyote's travel is symbolic. Of course, he has no power over the river, any more than over the liminality of—"

Ms. Beangurd: "Please, I think we can find a theme in these stories. Putting a story on the page implies decisions about its organization. The running translation reads well, but the interlinear translation and Nez Perce text, which precede it, suggest a different organization, when considered in terms of what has been learned recently about oral narratives in the same region and elsewhere. The text appears to have, not three parts, as published, but five. These five parts begin and end at points that do not coincide with the paragraphs of the running translation. The paragraphs of the running translation are reasonable, but *ad hoc*. The alternative parts are inferred from the language of the original in terms of a general assumption about the shaping of oral narratives."

Prof. Snootwhistle: "The form is artificial, a technique of publishing. The stories weren't always written. They were told. They were meant to be told, around campfires and in the dark, to keep children still and amused. Coyote is a vulgar but sacred form of the trickster character that exists in many human cultures. The trickster is supposed to scandalize, to disgust—"

Dr. Roegrimes: "Hey, Ms Bengayed, why does Snotgristle always get to go first. He's a *hack*! Oh, Snorepistol, you deluded romantic hack. Beanguard, you ignorant scientist. Coyote is absurd. Yes—"

Ms. Beangurd: "Gentlemen please. Allow me to finish before—oh, really? Well, it is my turn.

The assumption in these stories is that narrators organize what they say by weaving together two threads. One has to do with what. The other has to do with how. The shape of the told story has to do with both. That is, a good narrator knows two kinds of sequencing. One sequence consists of what happens, indeed, what must happen if the telling is to count as an instance of a story. And, the other sequence consists of relationships among lines and groups of lines, relationships that must pattern in certain ways if the story is to count as well-told.

Until recently, study of oral narratives, such as those of Native Americans, focused mostly on the what. That was what could be studied by those unacquainted with the languages, or working with materials for which the original languages were not available. Observations as to characteristic ways of telling stories might be made, but did not much affect how stories were presented. Now it is possible to discern the how in a thoroughgoing way, a way that requires presenting stories in its terms. Such a way makes explicit recurrences and relations among elements. In effect, it makes it possible to see what someone versed in the original tradition could have heard. With a certain effort, we can learn something that narrators and audiences tacitly knew.

Such analysis of the how depends upon three principles.

The first is that oral narratives consist of spoken lines, which need not be equivalent to written sentences.

The second principle is that of verse; of course, that is a term for poetry. Oral narratives, then, are not prose at all, but poetry. Often enough they are not poetry in the familiar sense of having lines with internal measurement, that is, meter, as do the sung epic traditions of India, classical Greece, Egypt, Turkey, Slavic peoples, Anglo-Saxons, et cetera et cetera. It is an instance of what the great linguist and student of poetry, Rumen Gherkin, considered basic to all poetry, namely, 'equivalence.' With metrical verse, equivalence may be seen in terms of syllables alone, or syllables and stresses, alliteration, rhymes, sequences of types of feet, et cetera et cetera.

The third—"

Dr. Roegrimes: "Thank you, now let me just say—boring!—"

Prof. Snootwhistle: "Oh, for Christ's sake, blow it out your ass."

Dr. Roegrimes: "You mean Deer's sake, sake-breath?"

Prof. Snootwhistle: "Or Coyote's sake, whatever. It should be noted that this whole "trickster" character and theme has been invented by scholars in the United States in order to characterize certain types of aboriginal mythical and folkloristic beings. In their own languages, native peoples of archaic cultures do not have particular terms for the kind of figure who transcends one culture.

The Algonquin's have a "cheat and liar." The Cree have a "deceiver." But, these terms cannot be analyzed into the same trickster. What we have is just another academic invention that is roughly straight-jacketed around many cultures. It is universal human ingenuity to posit tricksters. Possibly tricksters are evolving as consciousness evolves. Probably, there will be more feminine tricksters as women trumpet their equality. It can't be bad—"

Ms. Beangurd: "What about the ending? Does that mean that there is another trickster on the loose? The eternal feminine unleashed?"

Prof. Snootwhistle: "I just said that—Beargord?"

A quiet laugh, then there was silence.

About the author, *violet reason*, obviously a name used
to protect a reputation earned in a
different field of activity in the mainstream
of the unstoppable machine—anything else you
need to know about her can be found through her writings.

Violet Reason told me that she started writing coyote stories
when she was vacationing in Maine woods in summer 1988. She
was using her camera to take pictures of anything that moved,
mostly birds, but then she noticed a frog in the leaves. She got on
her knees and elbows to photograph the frog, but every time she
focused the frog stopped, and she could no longer see it on the
leaves and grasses. Soon she was crawling on knees and elbows
trying to click on the frog. She sensed a presence behind her and
whirled with the camera, to catch a golden brown coyote running
up the hill, looking back at her. The picture was blurred, as were
the ones of the frog. She wondered what the coyote was thinking:
Curiosity, butt-sniffing, mating, learning, or dinner? She always
laughed and blushed whenever she told the story. And, she tried
to understand Coyote as an animal and a mythical being. —YLL

About the Co-author, *Yulalona Lopez*: Harvard education in
astronomy, an associate of the Tohono O'odham people, an
independent investor, an amateur naturalist who has studied
coyotes and wolves—someone who speaks for the ultrahuman—
and a burgeoning author of *Tropomorphoses* and *Night Wolves*.
She says: "Mostly, when I read other poets, I think that they didn't
study enough astronomy, didn't get their knees scratched trying
to follow earthworms, haven't caught cold watching it snow on
their hands, haven't shaped their body to the bole of a tree or
crawled along a deer path through thickets—bend or become
still or small. I want to speak to these experiences." —AMC

Dedications

To the Coyote *Being* behind every coyote being.

To *Precious Woulfe*, who was able to offer joy and understanding to every living being.

To *Margaret Ryan*, who reads everything critically, but with amusement and encouragement.

And, to *Devorah Levy*, who suggested calamities that Coyote could cause at Mouseworld.

Finally to our soon-to-be-named, later-loyal readers.

—AMC & YLL

Colophon
Started on the Maine coast in the Summer of 1988.
Composed in Sabino canyon in the upper Sonoran desert
on a blue Ibook in the blue oak bus in the 1990s
using Gill Sans type text and Galliard display.
Graphics by Ryan Garcia Calusa
Cover: Aztec "Ueuecoyotl" or "Old Coyote"
Back cover: Aztec "Chachalaca" or "roadrunner"
Images of Blueworm, Buzzard, Eagle, Flower, Kingfisher,
Landscape, Mushroom, Puma, Snake, Vulture, Wheat,
and Zuni mythical creatures from uncopyrighted sources.

Review by *Susan Cardinal Sleepwell*

This is a novel of terror and laughter, of bondage and explosion—a searing *masterpiece* of tortured pieces, sewn in the skein of a sow's purse, as the authors pursue fame with shocking intensity. Coyote is changed from a complex morally ambiguous figure into a cardboard commentator for the animal news channel. The text *pulsates* with nervous energy and undigested gas. It is a searing satire cooked on the flames of passionate purple prose, disposed of in a desert setting of unparalleled natural pulchritude.

Most of all, it is an absurdist *classic*, reveling in the stupidity of humans in dealing with the nobility of animals, the meaninglessness of war and consumption, and the importance of breathing and excreting. We follow Coyote on his journey in search of free sex and food. The trip is not confined within the conventions of a linear or coherent narrative. Coyote bounces all over recollections and information, inner feeling and outer action. This not only *challenges* our expectations of literary form, but it irritates the shit out of us. Coyote's credo of greed and aggrandizement is fueled by testosterone, but fooled by estrogen. That is Coyote's lament—he is too late to deflower the intact virgin of bankrupt global capitalism and too early to grope the youth of utopia.

The narrative style reflects the confusion of his remembering over many lifetimes, then of delving into the plasma regions of repressed feelings and animal lust. The long sentences act like interminable *bridges* between unpleasant ideas and poorly formed thoughtscapes of half-hearted insights into the human and nonhuman conditions, which get soaked by plasma.

This is a novel where gods walk among people, sleep with them, ruin them financially, then go on and laugh and play. The settings in the deserts of North America and New York reflect the shadowy haunts of the gods trapped in their own deserts of unbelief and minimal clean water. The old gods may be forgotten by name, but they still struggle to snuggle and be warm under the blanket of belief that has been tattered by the oil-soaked machinery of modern materialism. New gods, with the same bad habits, start to *form* out of a developing post-industrial unconsciousness.

Review by *Rosetta Stone Plush*

This book is a vast *encyclopedic* romp through time and space. Alas, it does not have enough energy to keep moving for many seconds, or enough mass to keep it from floating away into the vacuum of space. However, it is filled with completely unnecessary bits and pieces, which are unappetizing and indigestible. The authors are *magical* surrealists who create inviting alternate realities using x-rays of the body of human thought and expression. Unfortunately, overexposure to x-rays can be fatal, so read cautiously.

     Yet, this is ultimately a gentle *meditation* on the act of telling stories and the failure of the telling to be relevant or meaningful. Although the book loses its grounding in traditional native story-telling, it never finds its place in contemporary, televised cartoon images. It is just a weak testimony to the inarticulateness of animal suffering.

     This bald existential *inquiry* into the meaning of masking requires a careful, thoughtful reading, that challenges us to ignore the fundamental questions of existence and fun. Here the dry prose of philosophers is transformed into the wet poetry of an incontinent versifier. I *loved* it! You will, too.

Lightning Source UK Ltd.
Milton Keynes UK
UKHW021835091220
374919UK00016B/369

9 781518 768064